# THE WOMAN BEHIND THE BADGE

DELORES FOSSEN

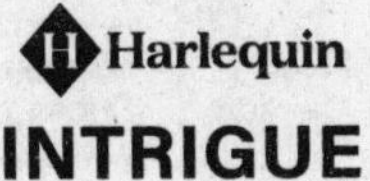

MIX
Paper | Supporting responsible forestry
FSC® C021394

Recycling programs for this product may not exist in your area.

ISBN-13: 978-1-335-69066-1

The Woman Behind the Badge



For questions and comments about the quality of this book, please contact us at CustomerService@Harlequin.com.

Harlequin Enterprises ULC
22 Adelaide St. West, 41st Floor
Toronto, Ontario M5H 4E3, Canada
www.Harlequin.com

HarperCollins Publishers
Macken House, 39/40 Mayor Street Upper,
Dublin 1, D01 C9W8, Ireland
www.HarperCollins.com

**Printed in Lithuania**

**He looked at her, their gazes colliding.**

Ethan must have seen that heat in her eyes. No way to shut it down, and over the years, Livvy had tried. Mercy, had she. Nothing had worked.

Normally, Ethan just turned away or quickly found an excuse to put some distance between them. But he didn't do that now. On a sigh, he pulled her into his arms.

"I can't be weak," she muttered. "I need to face this head-on."

"You are facing it," Ethan assured her. She felt his warm breath brush against her cheek. Almost a kiss. And, yes, that calmed her, too.

Along with giving her a tug of that heat.

But unwanted heat was far better than the stomach-twisting panic.

**Delores Fossen**, a *USA TODAY* bestselling author, has written over a hundred and fifty novels, with millions of copies of her books in print worldwide. She's received a Booksellers' Best Award and an RT Reviewers' Choice Best Book Award. She was also a finalist for a prestigious RITA® Award. You can contact the author through her website at www.deloresfossen.com.

## Books by Delores Fossen

### Harlequin Intrigue

#### *Renegade Canyon*

*Her Baby, Her Badge*
*Deputies Under Fire*
*Texas Baby Rescue*
*The Woman Behind the Badge*

#### *Saddle Ridge Justice*

*The Sheriff's Baby*
*Protecting the Newborn*
*Tracking Down the Lawman's Son*
*Child in Jeopardy*

#### *Silver Creek Lawman: Second Generation*

*Targeted in Silver Creek*
*Maverick Detective Dad*
*Last Seen in Silver Creek*
*Marked for Revenge*

#### *The Law in Lubbock County*

*Sheriff in the Saddle*
*Maverick Justice*
*Lawman to the Core*
*Spurred to Justice*

Visit the Author Profile page at Harlequin.com.

## CAST OF CHARACTERS

***Deputy Livvy Walsh***—She has no memory of the first six years of her life, but now that blank part of her past is threatening her life and her unborn child.

***Deputy Ethan Oakley***—He's the father of Livvy's baby, and his first priority is to protect them, but he's also battling the guilt he feels over his late wife's death.

***Vernice Cline***—Ethan's bitter former mother-in-law. She despises Ethan because she believes he should have stayed loyal to his late wife forever.

***Dr. Franklin Voss***—A fertility specialist and the codirector of the New Hope Wellness Center. He could be keeping dangerous secrets about Livvy's past.

***Chloe Voss***—Codirector of New Hope. She seems devastated over the murder of one of her employees, a murder that could be connected to Livvy, but Chloe's grief could be all a facade to cover her guilt.

***Anthony Carter***—He blames New Hope for his mother's death, and he's on a mission to learn the truth about what happened to her. But how far is he willing to go to get justice for her?

# *Chapter One*

It was the nightmare. But Deputy Livvy Walsh wasn't dreaming. She was wide awake, on the job.

And the nightmare was right here, right in front of her.

Livvy gasped, staggering back a step. She couldn't breathe, couldn't take her eyes off the blond-haired woman lying in the rust-streaked claw-foot tub. She was dead—no doubts about that. There wasn't a drop of color on her skin. But there was plenty of color on the sides of the tub and floor.

Blood.

Lots of it.

It pooled around the tub, the only item left in what had once been a bathroom in the abandoned house. Now the wood floor was warped and splintered, and the walls bore the holes from where other fixtures and such had been ripped out over the more than two decades since the place had been abandoned.

Definitely not a spot where someone would have settled in to take a long soak in the bath.

The back of the woman's neck was resting against the curved rim of the tub, but her head was turned toward the door. Toward Livvy. Her left arm was dangling over the side of the tub, her hand nearly touching the floor. A bead of blood had dried on the tip of her index finger, and judging from the pool beneath it, this had been her position when she had bled out.

Livvy swallowed hard and tried to tamp down her heart rate, her breathing. She was nearly five months pregnant, and she had to calm down for the sake of her baby.

She had managed to steady herself some, but she got another hit of adrenaline when she heard the footsteps behind her. Livvy automatically drew her gun and whirled around, expecting some part of the nightmare she'd never been able to see. A part that terrified her even more than the dream itself.

"Whoa," the man said when he saw her defensive stance.

Not the nightmare but rather her fellow deputy, Ethan Oakley. Of course, Ethan was more than that.

Way more.

He'd been a friend since childhood during their days at the Horseshoe Foster Ranch. He was also her partner at the Renegade Canyon Sheriff's Office.

And he was the father of her unborn child.

But other than the one time Ethan and she had been *together*, he wasn't her lover. She definitely wasn't the love of his life either. Not even close. That distinction belonged to his late wife, and Livvy was certain no other woman, including herself, would ever usurp that place of honor in his heart.

Still there were times, in those unguarded moments, that Ethan looked at her with heat sizzling in his gray eyes. Usually just as fast, he could shut it right down. But there was no heat now. Just a huge amount of concern.

"Whoa," he repeated, touching her hand to lower her gun. "The rest of the house is empty, but I'm guessing..."

Ethan's words trailed off as his gaze slid from her to the tub. And he cursed.

In a blink, he seemed to take in the entire room, including the dead woman. *Especially* the dead woman. Then his attention snapped back to her.

"It's your nightmare," he muttered.

Of course he knew about that. Best friends and all. And being a best friend and having a room just up the hall from hers at the Horseshoe Foster Ranch, Ethan had ended up rushing into her bedroom more than once to try to soothe her when the night terrors came.

Terrors filled with images of a dead blonde woman in a tub.

Blood everywhere. So much blood. And the woman's lifeless blue eyes fixed on Livvy.

The dream had been with Livvy as long as she could remember. Since she'd been six years old and had been found wandering around the small ranching town of Renegade Canyon, Texas. There'd been blood on her hands and clothes. But Livvy had had no idea how it'd gotten there. In fact, she'd had no idea of anything. The first six years of her life were simply a blank.

They still were.

"Come with me," Ethan insisted, slipping his arm around her waist, pulling her to him so that her face was buried against his chest. No doubt to shield her from seeing the body again.

He rarely touched her. Not since five months ago when they'd landed in bed and she'd gotten pregnant. And that told her just how awful she must've looked for him to have risked that kind of close contact. They'd learned the hard way that touching led to...other things. Things that she knew caused Ethan so much grief. It was the reason that Livvy usually refrained from touching him as well.

Clearly, though, this was an exception.

Livvy wasn't even sure she could move on her own, and she very much wanted to step out of this nightmare. Ethan helped with that. He led her back into the living room, such that it was. It was as dilapidated as the rest of the house, but at least there was no blood here. No dead woman.

*Out of sight* didn't mean *out of mind* though.

No. The images kept repeating in her head—the dead woman she'd just seen and the one who haunted her dreams.

"Wait here," Ethan insisted, moving away from her and taking out his phone.

She heard him call dispatch to alert the sheriff, Grace Granger, that they had a dead body and not the vandalism that the anonymous caller had reported. Ethan and Livvy had responded to the call, not expecting it to amount to anything.

They definitely hadn't believed they'd be stepping into a nightmare.

Hearing Ethan speak to dispatch gave Livvy a much-needed jolt. Not from the too-familiar images of the dead woman in the tub but rather a reminder that she had a job to do here. Another reminder that this wasn't a nightmare come to life. Someone was dead, and soon other responders would arrive. More cops, the CSIs and the EMTs, though the latter would only be for the sake of protocol. The woman was dead; she needed a medical examiner, not someone to give attention to those injuries.

"Grace will be out here in fifteen to twenty minutes," Ethan relayed to Livvy once he'd finished his call.

"Fifteen to twenty," Livvy had to repeat to get the words to sink in.

It was so hard to think, to settle her mind, but the short time frame meant the sheriff would be getting here as fast as possible. The ten-mile stretch between this house and Renegade Canyon was a narrow, curvy road, where it was next to impossible to speed. There must have been something in Ethan's voice that conveyed the urgency here to Grace.

And not merely the urgency of a dead body.

After all, there was nothing they could do to save the woman in the tub. It was obvious she'd been dead for hours, maybe even a day or two. But Grace was likely concerned about having a pregnant deputy at the scene where there could still be a killer around.

That reminder of a possible killer still in the area gave Livvy another jolt, and she did something she should have already done. She made a sweeping glance around the house to see if she could spot any clues to help them understand what'd happened here.

"Did you see anything suspicious when you checked the rest of the house?" she asked Ethan.

"No," he was quick to reply.

Ethan stared at her, studying her. No doubt making sure she wasn't about to lose it.

That was the only downside to being pregnant. Sometimes people treated her as if she were fragile and might shatter. Livvy wouldn't do that. Not just because of the effect it could have on her precious baby, but also because she was a cop.

A cop with serious emotional baggage, yes.

But the badge was important to her. And she could still do her job, now and after she had the baby. Doing that job meant dealing with this crime scene even if it was a trigger for that baggage.

"I need to look at the bathroom again," Livvy managed to say.

"I can do that," Ethan volunteered.

There it was again—that fragile stuff. "Thanks," she said. "But I need to see it for myself. For the report I'll have to do."

Ethan sighed and scratched the dark stubble on his jaw. Stubble that was always there and made him look a little like an Old West outlaw. After a few moments of hesitation, he finally motioned for her to follow him. She did, all the while keeping watch around them.

Livvy took a deep breath, then a second one, before they stepped into the bathroom. She didn't look at the woman again. Not yet. Instead, she focused on the room itself.

"No visible footprints," she muttered. "Just smears." Possibly caused by someone dragging something—like a body. Or by someone purposely trying to obliterate any evidence by raking something through the prints.

"No clothes either," Ethan pointed out.

True. And the woman was naked. Which could mean two things: Either the woman had come here naked—not a strong possibility since it was chilly outside and there wasn't a vehicle found in the vicinity of the house—or whoever put her in the tub had also taken her clothes.

Watching where he stepped, Ethan went closer to the tub, but Livvy stayed put. The only way she could do her job right now was to focus on the scene and not the dead woman.

"I believe she's been stabbed in the chest and stomach," Ethan said.

His back was to Livvy now, but she saw the rise of his

wide, strong shoulders as he took his own deep breath. Like her, Ethan had been a cop for nearly twelve years, and while they hadn't seen a ton of dead bodies, they had certainly seen more than their fair share.

"We need to go outside and look around," he suggested, tipping his head to the window. Like some of the walls, it was a wide-open hole with the glass and the frame long gone.

Livvy understood the need for them to check for a vehicle or any evidence that should be preserved, but she suspected Ethan was also eager to get her out of this room. To put a little distance between her and this visual nightmare.

She felt as if she had gone on autopilot as she followed Ethan outside into the cold, damp air. The air was equally cold and damp inside as well, but at least with the brisk November-morning breeze, there wasn't the smell of blood.

They made their way through what had once been a side yard, careful of each step. Mindful, too, of their surroundings. This part of Texas was renowned for its beautiful views and limestone bluffs, but there wasn't much beautiful about the land that surrounded the one-story wood-frame house.

Nature had reclaimed most of the yard so that it was now just weeds and what was left of a decaying picket fence. What Livvy didn't see were any of those weeds trampled. And they likely would have been had someone recently walked through here.

She glanced across the gravel-and-dirt road and saw the field of dead cornstalks. Acres of them. There were no other houses in sight, but she made a mental note to find the owner of the property to check if he or she had seen anything out of the ordinary.

"How close does this come to matching your nightmare?" Ethan asked, and she could hear the hesitancy in his question. Maybe he thought talking about it would just keep it fresh in her mind.

But it was *always* on her mind.

"Very close," she admitted. "The woman's face is different, but the hair color is the same. Ditto for the way she's positioned in the tub." She glanced around, frowned. "Actually, this feels familiar, too."

He stopped and turned to her, and the concern was all over his face. "Are you…remembering?"

She was quick to shake her head. "I'm not sure the recurring nightmare has anything to do with my past."

But the odds were that it did. It was likely that she had experienced something. Some kind of hell that no six-year-old kid should ever have to experience.

Ethan made a sound that could have meant anything and got them moving again. "I think you should sit out this investigation." He glanced at her stomach, and while he didn't come out and say *Think of the baby*, she thought that was what he meant.

Livvy wanted to sit it out. Mercy, did she. She wanted to distance herself from what she'd seen in that bloody bathtub. She wanted to shove it all aside and never see those images again.

But that wasn't going to happen.

The images were there now, and while it wasn't something she could explain, the dead woman felt like her responsibility. And maybe that hadn't been by accident.

"You and I are the only deputies in the station at this time of morning," Livvy said.

Not super early. It was already eight. But it'd be another hour before a third deputy came in. Grace would have no doubt called to have that deputy come in to cover her or else left the dispatcher in charge so she could make the trip here.

"And you think—what?" he asked. "That the anonymous call was specifically meant to get you here to this place, to see that body?"

He made it sound a little far-fetched, but it didn't feel that way to Livvy. This felt like some kind of setup. A taunt or a trigger. Something designed to rattle her to the core.

But why?

And better yet, who would do that?

Those questions repeated in her mind as they made their way to the back of the house. Still no sign of a vehicle, but Livvy spotted something: The weeds here had indeed been trampled on. The makeshift trail went from the porch to the woods behind the house.

Livvy slid her hand over her weapon again. Ethan did the same, and they both peered out into the thick trees and shrubs. She didn't see anyone, but a sound caught her attention.

A sort of rustling.

At first, she thought it was the breeze teasing the dead leaves that remained on some of the trees. But the sound had come from her right, and Livvy pivoted there.

And she saw the piece of paper on the back door.

The wind was having a go at it, and the bottom was flapping around, threatening to rip off the single nail that was holding it in place. The paper wasn't weathered but rather crisp and white. Definitely something that had been recently placed here.

Keeping an eye on their surroundings, they went closer and cautiously made their way up the rickety steps. There was no blood here but more of those smears as if someone had wanted to make sure they'd left no footprints behind.

"Hell," Ethan muttered when they were finally close enough to the paper.

She didn't say anything. Couldn't. Because her throat had suddenly clamped shut. *Oh, God.*

The words practically jumped off the paper at her.

*Livvy, it's time you remembered. Time for you to confess that you're a killer.*

# *Chapter Two*

Ethan set the cup of water on the desk next to Livvy. "Drink this," he insisted.

He seriously doubted that mere water was going to put any color back in Livvy's cheeks. Or eliminate that shock he was seeing in her pale green eyes. In fact, nothing might help with that, but he had to try anyway.

This wasn't about the stress that her anxiety was putting on the baby. It was about Livvy herself. They might not have been the best of friends as they once were, and he might've felt the guilt from hell just looking at her, but Ethan hated to see her hurting like this.

And she was hurting, no doubt about it.

All thanks to the blasted note that had shaken her to the core. It'd shaken him, too, but Ethan was trying to push it aside and help Livvy deal with…well, whatever the heck this was.

"The note could be a lie, meant to taunt you," he pointed out. Not for the first time. He'd said as much in the cruiser when Grace had told them to leave the crime scene, return to the station and wait for her in her office. But now Ethan added more. "As a cop, you've made enemies, and one of them might want to hurt you."

If that was it, then the enemy had succeeded.

*Livvy, it's time you remembered. Time for you to confess that you're a killer.*

Yeah, definitely a success.

Because of the best-friends deal that had started when they were both six and in foster care, Ethan knew how much her blank past haunted her. Or a better word for it might've been *terrorized* her. Not just the nightmares but those empty spaces inside her that should've been filled with memories and certain knowledge.

But she didn't have that.

In fact, even her name was something that'd been given to her by the foster care system after they hadn't been able to identify her or locate any possible kin. Now she had to be imagining the worst-possible scenarios for those blanks.

That she was a killer.

That at age six, she had ended someone's life.

"You need to make a list," Ethan said, trying again to get her to focus on anything but those blank spots, the dead woman and the note. "Write down anyone you think might want to get back at you by doing something like this."

He took a notepad from Grace's desk and dropped it and a pen next to the cup of water. Livvy finally looked up at him. "You think someone murdered a woman to get back at me?"

"It's possible," he had to admit. "But there are many reasons the woman could have been killed."

She drank some water and nodded. "But one of the reasons for her murder could point right back to me," Livvy said, and her voice cracked. "I didn't kill her, Ethan."

He looked at her as if she'd just told him she was an alien from Mars. "Hell, Livvy. I know that." Ethan groaned and put his hands on his hips.

"But will everyone else believe it?" she asked.

And there it was. Something he hadn't considered. The worry that because of that note, people would think she was a killer.

Ethan leaned down, took hold of her shoulders and looked her straight in the eyes. "No one who knows you will think you killed that woman."

She stared at him as if trying to detect any doubts about that. There wouldn't be any. He knew her down to her soul, and the only reason that best friends' bond no longer applied was because of him. Because of the mistake he'd made landing in bed with her on the first anniversary of his wife's death.

Isabel's death.

He'd been in such a dark place that night. The grief had been eating him alive, and he'd turned to Livvy. The grief was still there and felt as if it always would be, but he now had a mountain of guilt to go along with it. Guilt over "betraying" his late wife and twisting Livvy's life to hell and back by getting her pregnant.

Oh, she wanted this baby. He had no doubts about that either. He wanted it as well. But that didn't mean it hadn't given them both the unplanned upheaval of becoming parents. Parents who were both haunted by their pasts.

Ethan realized his gaze was still locked with Livvy's. And that he still had hold of her shoulders. Was very close to her. So close that he felt that blasted heat stir in him. He practically snapped back, putting some much-needed distance between them.

Livvy continued to stare at him a moment later, and then she seemed to steel herself up. "The list," she repeated, picking up a pen. "I'll focus on what I can do to help with the investigation."

"Good. I'll do the same."

And he took out his phone to try to chase down some preliminary reports of the crime scene. Later, he'd be doing his own list because anyone who wanted to get back at him might use Livvy to dole out some punishment.

Ethan had barely gotten started on his search when he heard the approaching footsteps, and several moments later, Grace came in. Even though it was barely ten o'clock, she already looked exhausted and headed straight for her coffeemaker. She poured herself a huge cup and offered them one.

Both Livvy and he declined.

Grace had a long sip of her coffee and dropped down into her chair behind her desk. "I won't ask how you're holding up," she said, aiming that at Livvy. "I can see you're shaken. Do you want to talk about that or get on with what I have to tell you about the investigation?"

"The investigation," Livvy replied without a second of hesitation.

Ethan could already tell that she was shaking off the shock and she was in the full cop mode now. Good. Because he figured these next few minutes—hell, the entire case—was going to add another level to her night terrors.

"All right." Grace nodded. "Here's what we know. The dead woman is Zadie Covington."

Livvy muttered the name as if testing it to see if it rang any bells. She shook her head. Ethan had to do the same. He'd never heard of her, and he was certain he'd never seen her before either.

"She died from bleeding out from multiple stab wounds," Grace added.

"Self-inflicted?" Ethan asked.

"Probably not. The ME will give us a determination on that soon though." She paused, had more coffee and pulled up some notes on her phone. "We got a quick hit on identifying because her prints are in the system from a DUI she got a couple of years back. She was thirty-one and was born in San Antonio. No marriage on record, no kids. She was a certified nursing assistant, and her last known address is the New Hope Wellness Center."

Everything inside Ethan went still. Because that facility was familiar to him. It was located about five miles from town and specialized in fertility treatments. Well, unconventional treatments anyway. Ethan had always figured the powers-that-be there preyed on women desperate to have a child.

That included his late wife.

"Isabel went there about six months before she died," Ethan volunteered. "I didn't go with her," he added.

More guilt. More regret. If he'd gone with Isabel, she might not have been so desperate to try other measures to conceive. And since one of those measures had led to a stroke and then her death, Ethan wished he had something, anything, so that he didn't feel as if he'd failed her.

Grace nodded, responding to what Ethan had said. "I'll obviously need to go out to New Hope and have a chat with them," she let them know.

"I can do that," Livvy and he said practically at the same time.

Grace sipped more coffee and eyed them, no doubt trying to decide if that was a good move. "All right," she finally agreed, "but let's go over some things first. Tell me about that note. What do you think it means?"

Ethan wanted to blurt out an explanation, but this wasn't his story to tell. It was Livvy's.

Livvy drank more of the water before she spoke. "Since I was a kid….since I was found at age six, I've had a recurring nightmare. A dead blond-haired woman in a bathtub. Lots of blood. Old house out in the sticks." She swallowed hard. "That crime scene pretty much nailed my nightmare."

Grace stared at her a moment. "I see. But you don't know if you actually saw that scene before today or if it's just a bad dream?"

"No," Livvy assured her. "And I'm not sure why the note said I was a killer. I certainly don't recall killing anyone, not even in the line of duty and especially not when I was six years old."

Grace would have only been ten or so at the time Livvy was found, but she would likely recall the little girl who the sheriff had found wandering on the road into Renegade Canyon. She had also likely heard about Livvy being found with blood on her. But since no body or anyone injured had ever been found, that blood was essentially a twenty-eight-year-old mystery.

Of course, other things were a twenty-eight-year-old mystery, too. Including her name. Livvy, or rather Olivia, was what CPS had given her when she'd entered foster care. The Walsh surname had apparently been plucked out of thin air. Better than calling her Jane Doe, Ethan supposed.

"Who knows about this nightmare you have?" Grace asked.

Livvy glanced at him. "Ethan. He experienced the aftermath of it plenty of times. And Eden," she added, referring to their fellow deputy Eden Gallagher, who'd also been raised at the Horseshoe Foster Ranch. "The half dozen or so doctors and therapists I've seen over the years. Oh, and your mother."

Grace clearly wasn't surprised by that. Her mother, Aileen, had been sheriff for several decades before she retired, and she'd been the one who'd actually found Livvy. Throughout the years that followed, Aileen had checked on Livvy often, and Ethan had been there when Livvy had told Aileen about the nightmares.

But Aileen wasn't a suspect here.

Even though she no longer carried a badge, Aileen was a cop to the bone, and she'd never do anything to hurt Livvy.

"I'll want the names of everyone, including those doctors and therapists, who knew about the specific details of the dreams," Grace spelled out. "That includes any of your former foster siblings."

Livvy nodded, and while she looked as if she was totally in control, Ethan noticed her hand tremble a little when she started writing.

"The person who killed Zadie Covington might or might not be the same person who left that note," Grace went on. "But we have to consider that they're one and the same. And that this is probably someone from your past."

"A past I can't remember," Livvy muttered. She wrote down some names, the point of the pen digging so hard into the paper that it risked ripping it. "And that someone from my past could have wanted me to see that scene. Could have made sure I did." She paused. "Can we trace the caller who reported the vandalism?"

Grace sighed in frustration and shook her head. "It was made from a burner."

That surprised none of them. If the person had wanted his or her identity known, it wouldn't have been anonymous.

"And yeah, the caller was almost certainly the killer and the person who wanted you there at that house," Grace admitted. "Since we can't trace it, we have to work the details that we do have. Maybe the CSIs will turn up something at the house. Or the ME can find some trace evidence on the body."

Ethan hoped something would turn up. Something that would essentially clear Livvy's name.

"SAPD did the death notification to Zadie's parents, but I want to drive over and talk to them," Grace continued. "You two deal with New Hope. Someone there might know what happened to her."

That was Livvy's and his cue to get moving out the door. Ethan had no idea if Livvy was ready for this ordeal. Probably anything and everything connected to this case would trigger the hellish images from the dream and the actual scene. But he figured it was best to stay busy, and that way, they might get the answers they needed to solve this.

They stopped in the bullpen, and Livvy had to move the black cat off her jacket that was lying on her desk. The cat, Sherlock, was sort of a mascot and more or less had free rein of the place. He also had opinions and somehow managed to purr at Livvy and hiss at Ethan all in the same breath.

Despite everything, Livvy smiled. It was brief and the smile didn't reach her eyes, but he was glad she'd gotten a second or two of amusement.

It didn't last.

The moment they had their jackets on, they went toward the front door, but it opened before they even reached it. And Ethan immediately saw someone he didn't want to see: Vernice Cline. Isabel's mother and his former mother-in-law.

Since Vernice had had Isabel when she'd only been nineteen, she was still fairly young. Only fifty-three. And she appeared even younger than that with her gym-fit body and hair and makeup applied as if she were about to head to a fancy business meeting. Ethan doubted she had any such meetings on her agenda since she ran a pet-grooming business, but being dressed to a tee was Vernice's default.

Vernice scowled when her attention landed on him, but that scowl skyrocketed when she shifted her gaze to Livvy.

And the baby bump.

It was an expected reaction, and Ethan couldn't blame Vernice for her bitterness. Here, her beloved daughter had died trying to conceive a child, and it'd happened with Livvy and him in a one-off.

Of course, Vernice didn't believe it was a one-time occurrence, and she had often accused him of jumping straight into Livvy's bed instead of "honoring" Isabel's memory by remaining faithful to her.

Again, Ethan couldn't fault the woman for thinking that way. He was dealing with that same disgust for himself. That guilt which was made even stronger by the love he felt for his unborn child.

"You're together, I see," Vernice snarled.

"We're partners," Ethan reminded her, again.

Vernice's eyes narrowed. "That's your choice. You two want to be together. If you didn't, you could ask Grace to pair you up with someone else."

It was true. Grace would have switched them. And Ethan had considered it. Man, had he. But he'd finally decided that if he asked for another partner, that would cause tension in the police station. The other cops would walk on eggshells around Livvy and him, and that would hurt the job. Hell, it would hurt the entire department. So, by mutual agreement, they'd stayed together as partners.

"Vernice, we're on our way out," Ethan said, intending to cut this visit short. Then again, he always wanted to minimize his time with Vernice.

"Well, I wouldn't have come if it were up to me," the woman snapped, and she reached into her massive purse and yanked out a package that was about the size of child's shoebox. She thrust it at him. "When I went to open the shop this morning, that was on the doorstep. It's addressed to you, so I played messenger and brought it over. You're welcome," she tacked on with plenty of snark.

Ethan ignored her attitude and carefully took the package from her hand. "Why leave it at your shop?"

"I wouldn't know" was her frosty response. She gave Livvy's baby bump one last glare before she turned and walked out.

"What is that?" Grace asked.

He glanced back and saw the sheriff was walking toward them, and judging from her expression, she had probably overheard at least some of the conversation with Vernice.

Ethan had to shake his head. "I've never gotten any deliveries or mail at Vernice's shop."

With Livvy right next to her, he went back into the bullpen and eased the package onto his desk. He took out a pair of latex gloves and the explosives scanner while he studied the writing. No sender info, no addresses.

Just his name, Deputy Ethan Oakley.

Beneath that were three words: *Important. Open Immediately.*

Ethan didn't open it *immediately*. Instead, he ran the handheld scanner over the box. There was no telltale beep to let him know there might be a bomb, but the device did alert on something metal.

"Stand back just in case," he told Livvy and Grace, and

he waited for them to do that before he opened the package and peered inside.

Frowning, he spilled the contents onto his desk. A folded piece of paper and a six-inch knife encased in a layer of bubble wrap. He could see rust-colored smears on the blade.

He thought it might be dried blood.

"That could be the murder weapon," Grace speculated.

"Yeah," Ethan agreed, and he shifted his attention to the paper.

He carefully unfolded it and saw that it was a note. A note that had Ethan cursing.

*Test it, Deputy Oakley. You'll find Livvy's fingerprints on it. Maybe now she'll confess to everything she's done.*

# *Chapter Three*

Livvy stared at the words. And stared.

They carved into her like a blade—deep, sharp and unrelenting. Each one stripped away her breath, pressing on her chest until it felt like her lungs might cave in.

But she wouldn't let the crushing weight break the surface. Wouldn't give whoever wrote it that kind of power.

Not now. Not ever.

She locked her jaw, forced her spine straight as she repeated the message to herself: *Test it, Deputy Oakley. You'll find Livvy's fingerprints on it. Maybe now she'll confess to everything she's done.*

The taunt hit like a punch, but she didn't flinch. Didn't blink. Because she didn't just see a threat scrawled on that paper. She saw a challenge.

And she'd meet it head-on.

"Send it to the lab," Livvy insisted once she was able to gather enough breath to speak.

She turned to Grace, trying to let her boss see that while she was shaken, she was also determined to get to the bottom of this. Someone was clearly trying to rattle her or attempting to set her up for something, and Livvy wasn't just going to roll over and let that happen.

"I've never seen that knife before," she insisted.

It was the truth. Well, the truth as she knew it anyway. It was possible the knife was hidden in those blank spots in her memories. But Livvy knew for a fact that she didn't consciously recall seeing it. And she was certain that she would have remembered. The knife was distinctive with its bone handle that had an eagle carved into it.

Grace gave a slight nod, and while Livvy thought her boss believed her about not having ever seen the knife, Grace was no doubt assessing how to deal with this. Livvy spoke up, eager to try to keep herself involved in this investigation.

"Please don't make me sit out this case," she said, trying to look and sound as if this hadn't gotten to her. "I can help. In fact, I should help. If that woman died because of something that happened in my past, then I need to confront it head-on." She had to take a deep breath before she added, "And maybe the investigation will finally trigger the memories."

She wasn't at all certain she wanted that, but if these blank spots could solve a murder, then it had to be done. Until now, that amnesia was only affecting her and those who got caught up in her night terrors. However, if it was allowing a killer to go free, then the remembering had to be done.

Of course, the therapists and treatments over the years had all failed. But again, the stakes weren't as high as they were now. The memories could be crucial to catching a killer. And to clearing her own name since it was obvious that someone was trying to set her up with these blasted notes and the knife.

"Ethan and I can do this interview at New Hope," Livvy went on.

But then she paused and shifted to Ethan to make sure

that interview was okay with him. After all, New Hope might trigger some bad memories of Isabel since she'd visited there.

He studied her much as Grace had done, his gaze sliding over her face. No heat this time around. None of that unwanted attraction. Just a cop's assessment to make sure she was up to this.

Ethan finally nodded. "Yes, Livvy and I can go to New Hope."

Grace took a moment, then another, before she spoke. "All right, go, but if at any point you sense you're in danger, get the hell out of there."

Livvy had already considered the possibility of danger, but it was a jolt to hear it spelled aloud. It was indeed possible that someone wanted to hurt her or worse. That could be what these taunting notes were about. Still, if the person wanted her dead, then all he or she had needed to do was hang around that abandoned house and shoot her when she stepped from the cruiser.

Definitely not a comforting thought, but it was the truth. She would have had no idea that something like that was coming.

"Go," Grace finally said, "and on the drive over, run a background on New Hope. Let me know if any red flags pop."

"Will do," Ethan assured her.

They didn't waste any time heading out to the cruiser. As usual, she drove, and with Ethan at shotgun, he immediately took out his phone, no doubt to start that search on New Hope.

"I'm taking you at your word," he said, "that you're okay with doing this."

"I am. I'm taking you at your word, too."

"Good. Because we have a killer to catch," Ethan was quick to say. "New Hope," he went on a moment later, reading from his phone. "Established nearly forty years ago."

She hadn't known it'd been around that long, and since it wasn't exactly on the beaten path, Livvy hadn't even seen the place.

"Here's their mission statement," he continued a moment later. "'At New Hope, we are committed to empowering women on their journey to parenthood. Through compassionate care and personalized treatment plans here at our residential facility, we strive to provide hope and support to every individual or family facing fertility challenges.'"

"'Personalized treatment plans,'" she repeated. "Impressive sounding while also being vague. Does it say specifically what they offer?"

He scrolled through the screen and shook his head. Ethan also gathered his breath. "But I remember Isabel saying it wasn't actually fertility treatments. More like nutrition and exercise plans. The residential facility part was emphasized though. They want couples to actually live there while trying to conceive."

"Not very convenient," she muttered. "And it sounds expensive."

"It is," he assured her. "Not just for the stay and treatment but also for a surrogacy option."

"Surrogacy?" she questioned.

"Gestational surrogacy," Ethan provided. "The embryo of the couple implanted into a surrogate. That option requires at least one member of the couple and the surrogate to live at New Hope until the birth of the baby."

"Good grief," Livvy muttered. "That seems strict."

He made a sound of agreement. "And from what I gathered from Isabel, most clients ended up going the surrogacy route."

So, the place was making a fortune. Maybe. It was also possible they didn't get many clients.

"The director of New Hope is Chloe Voss," Ethan continued, reading from his phone. "Age fifty-eight. A nurse practitioner and nutritionist. No criminal record. Divorced." He paused. "No kids, which could mean…nothing, I suppose."

True. It was possibly Chloe simply hadn't wanted children, but then it seemed somewhat of an unusual career choice to run a facility dedicated to conception and childbirth. Still, helping others conceive a child didn't necessarily mean that you wanted them yourself.

"Her parents started New Hope," Ethan added a moment later, "and Chloe took over as director when her parents died about a decade ago. Her brother, Franklin, is a doctor at New Hope."

Livvy was processing all that info when her phone rang, and since it was already linked with Bluetooth, she saw the name on the dash screen.

And she groaned.

Because it was Dr. Millie Burnette. Her obstetrician. Definitely not a conversation she wanted to have with Ethan around, since he'd just been talking about Isabel. Still, this could be important, so she used hands-free and took the call.

"Livvy," the woman immediately greeted. Not the doctor but rather her nurse. "This is Delia at Dr. Burnette's office. We need to reschedule your ultrasound appointment and wondered if you could come in tomorrow at one?"

"Sure," Livvy said without even knowing what was on her calendar. But she didn't want to prolong this chat.

"Great. We'll see you then, and just remember—tell your technician if you don't want to know the gender of the baby."

"All right. Thanks," she blurted. Her tone must have conveyed to the nurse that this wasn't a good time for a chat because Delia said a friendly goodbye and ended the call.

"You don't have to go with me," Livvy offered.

"I'll go," he snapped.

Speaking of tones, his conveyed what she'd thought it would. Ethan wasn't happy about this appointment, but he would absolutely go just as he'd done with all her other ones. And his gruff voice and expression had nothing to do with his feelings for their baby. He loved this child. Livvy knew that. But with love came guilt, and Ethan was practically drowning in it.

It was the same for Livvy.

Isabel had been her friend, too, and it felt like a betrayal to have slept with Ethan. At least now it did. At the time, with the heat and need dictating, well, everything...being with him had felt like a necessity.

Thankfully, Ethan and she didn't have to discuss the appointment or anything else because Livvy took the turn to New Hope. The place wasn't visible from the main road, but once she got past massive groves of pecan and oak trees, she spotted the house.

It wasn't a modern-looking clinic but rather a sprawling Victorian house. It had obviously been well maintained with its yellow exterior and white shutters. That applied to the yard, too, which looked like something right out of an English gardening magazine.

Even though it was practically winter, there were clay pots filled with colorful flowers on the wraparound porch. Plenty of seating, too, with carefully arranged wicker rocking chairs. It looked welcoming and peaceful, which was no doubt a necessity to appeal to the wealthy clients who might end up staying here.

Livvy studied the house and grounds to see if anything felt familiar. It didn't. Not like that feeling she'd gotten at the abandoned house where they'd found Zadie. She had that sickening déjà vu there.

"No vehicles in sight," Ethan commented, drawing her attention back to him.

Yes, and that added to the picture-perfect look of the place. Livvy spotted a large barn, also well kept, at the back of the house and figured that it might be used as a garage.

Still glancing around, they got out and made their way to the door, but before they could ring the bell, it opened. A tall woman with silver-gray hair stared at them. She wasn't wearing scrubs or a white medical coat but was instead in loose navy pants and a matching top. Like the house and the grounds, she didn't look familiar to Livvy.

The woman's eyes were red, and she was dabbing at tears with a wadded-up tissue. She forced a smile that faltered completely when her gaze landed on Livvy's baby bump.

"Oh," she said. "I was expecting a new client who's trying to conceive, but it's obvious you're not her. Congratulations." She thrust out her hand before Livvy could respond. "I'm Chloe Voss, the director of New Hope. I'm afraid you've come at a bad time. We've just gotten some horrible news."

So, she knew about Zadie. Either that or something else bad had happened to bring on those tears.

"I'm Deputy Ethan Oakley, and this is my partner, Deputy Livvy Walsh, from Renegade Canyon Sheriff's Office," he explained. "We're here to talk to you about Zadie Covington."

Chloe gave a resigned nod and stepped back so they could enter. "Her mother just called me. Apparently a cop came to her door and told her, and she didn't want to believe it. She wanted me to tell her that Zadie was here. Alive and safe." Her bottom lip trembled. "But instead I had to explain that I hadn't seen Zadie since the end of her shift yesterday."

"When was that?" Livvy asked.

"At five p.m." Chloe motioned for them to follow her, and she led them out the impressive foyer and just up a hall into a sitting room or maybe a library. "Most of the staff lives here on the third floor," she explained, tipping her head in the direction of the stairs, "and I assumed Zadie was in her quarters since she wasn't due to come back on duty until noon today. It's her half day," she added.

"Any idea when Zadie left New Hope?" Ethan pressed.

"None." She paused, blinked back more tears, and her gaze shifted to a heavily pregnant woman in a coat who was strolling through the side garden. "There's no curfew or anything, and since Zadie's car is still in the barn, I assume someone picked her up. And no, I don't have any idea who would have done that—" She stopped, and her forehead bunched up. "That's not true. I do have an idea. It's possible that Anthony came and got her."

"Anthony?" Livvy took out her phone to make note of the name.

"Anthony Carter." Now some irritation or even anger

flashed in her dark brown eyes. "Zadie's ex-boyfriend. They had a bad breakup last week, and I thought she was done with him. Maybe not though. He could have possibly sweet-talked her into going with him and arranged to pick her up at the end of the road."

Or he could have used some kind of force to make her go with him. Yes, they'd be looking into this Anthony Carter, and Livvy got started on that by texting Grace to let her know about him. The sheriff would get him in for an interview right away.

Another pregnant woman walked by the window, moving toward the one already in the garden. "How many people live here?" Livvy wanted to know. "And we'll need names."

Chloe nodded. "We have five clients." She tipped her head to the two outside. "The brunette is Hannah Brooks, and Leah Parker is the redhead. They're surrogates. Hannah is carrying a baby for Charlotte Winslow, and Leah for Sienna Carrington. Sienna's husband, David, lives here as well, but he's away on a business trip."

She continued listing clients, and Livvy wrote them all down. "And the staff? How many?"

"Five who live here," Chloe said and then stopped again. "Four," she amended, her voice wobbling when she mentally took Zadie off her list. "The housekeeper and cook, Veronica Baskar. My assistant, Sunny. My brother, Dr. Franklin Voss, and then me. We also have a groundskeeper part-time—Buddy Jenkins—but he doesn't live here."

They would need to speak to all of them, but for now, she needed the basics. "What's Sunny's surname?" Livvy asked.

"Covington," Chloe replied as if the answer was obvious. "She's, uh, Zadie's sister."

Ethan and Livvy exchanged a glance, and it was Ethan who voiced what they needed. "If she's here, we have to talk to her *now*." A sister was far more likely than a boss to know personal details that could have led to Zadie's murder.

Chloe nodded and then reached over and pressed a button on a discreet-looking intercom on the end table. "Sunny, could you please come to the front parlor? The police are here."

"Yes" was the woman's barely audible reply.

"Uh, please go easy on her," Chloe whispered. "Sunny and Zadie were very close."

She'd barely gotten out the last word when there was the sound of rushing footsteps. Someone was flat-out running toward the room, and it put Livvy and Ethan on full alert. They adjusted their positions so it'd be easier to get to their weapons. They soon realized it wasn't a threat.

But it was a shock.

The woman who ran into the room had a tear-streaked face with identical features to Zadie's.

Livvy choked back a gasp, barely, but she couldn't stop the flashbacks of seeing a dead Zadie in that tub. So much like her nightmare with that blond hair and pale skin. Sunny was blonde and pale, too, but this living, breathing woman wasn't identical to the one from Livvy's dreams. Close but not a perfect match.

"I forgot to mention that Sunny and Zadie are identical twins," Chloe said, obviously noticing Livvy's reaction. "It must have startled you to see Sunny."

"It did," she admitted.

"Is Zadie really dead?" Sunny asked. "I mean, I know what the cops told Mom, but is she really dead?"

"Yes," Livvy verified.

"Sit down, Sunny," Chloe coaxed, taking her by the hand and easing Sunny onto the sofa next to her. "These are deputies from Renegade Canyon, and they have some questions for you. They need to find out who hurt your sister."

*Hurt*. That was a mild way of putting it, but Livvy didn't correct her. Sunny looked as if she was barely hanging on by a thread, and it was best to make this fast and as gentle as possible. It certainly wouldn't help if she knew the bloody details of her sister's murder.

"When's the last time you saw your sister?" Livvy started.

Sunny pulled in a long, trembling breath. "Last night… around seven or so. She came to my suite to borrow some nail polish remover. I was working on budget reports, and I didn't even really talk to her other than to tell her to help herself to the polish remover. She didn't say anything about going out," she added in a mutter.

But she had done exactly that. Maybe not voluntarily though. "Do you have any idea when and why your sister left New Hope?" Livvy asked.

"No," Sunny was quick to say, and she looked at her boss. "Did you tell them about Anthony?"

Chloe nodded. "I'm sure they'll talk to him."

"Talk to him and arrest him," Sunny spat out, some of her grief and shock replaced by anger. "Because he did this."

All right. This Anthony was now top priority, and he'd need to be brought in for questioning.

"Tell me about Anthony," Livvy prompted. "And about their breakup."

Sunny took a couple of moments, clearly fighting to keep hold of her composure. "I think he was some kind of con artist. I caught him in a couple of lies. Nothing major, but I thought if he'd lie about little things, he'd probably lie about bigger ones, too."

"For instance?" Ethan pressed.

"Like saying he'd never been here to New Hope, but he knew about the old root cellar. He made a joke about it. And he mentioned the house used to be a different color." Sunny lifted her shoulder. "Little things," she repeated in a mutter and then fell silent.

Livvy didn't answer right away. Her mind was already racing, latching onto every detail. Little things. That was what predators got caught on—details they didn't mean to drop, slips they didn't think mattered.

But they mattered to Livvy.

Her gut stirred, sharp and uneasy. She knew those kinds of inconsistencies weren't just forgettable quirks. They were cracks in a carefully built lie. And she'd learned, sometimes the hard way, to never ignore those cracks.

She narrowed her eyes slightly, gaze settling on the horizon, but her thoughts were miles ahead. If he was lying about never being here, what else was Anthony hiding? And why?

Livvy pressed her palm against her belly, grounding herself. Then she looked at Sunny again. "How did Zadie meet him, and how long were they together?"

"She met him about three months ago, when he came here to New Hope to write an article. He's a blogger and does stories about unique businesses and buildings in Texas." Sunny's voice cracked, and she paused again.

"Zadie and he started dating shortly thereafter, and they ended things about a week ago."

"Why?" Livvy had to know.

Sunny shook her head. "Zadie refused to say, but he broke her heart—I could tell. So, he must have done something so despicable that she didn't want to let me in on it. Maybe because she was too embarrassed or because she thought I'd go after him and make him pay for hurting my sister. Zadie doesn't have a temper, but I do."

Livvy could definitely see the anger, but at the moment, grief was winning the emotional battle. If Sunny had had anything to do with her sister's death, she was certainly putting on an award-winning performance.

"Would Zadie have left here with Anthony last night?" Ethan asked.

"I wouldn't think so." Sunny's gaze slashed to Chloe. "Would she?" There was a plea in her voice. She didn't want that possibility to be true.

"I don't know," Chloe admitted.

"She could have gone with him," Sunny murmured, and she got to her feet. "I'm sorry. I can't do this now. I just can't do this," she insisted, and she hurried out of the room.

Livvy and Ethan didn't go after her, but they would have to question her more. Sunny might have vital information to ID her sister's killer. But Chloe might as well.

"Other than Anthony is there anyone else who might have wanted to harm Zadie?" Livvy came out and asked.

When Chloe shook her head, Livvy added, "Maybe a disgruntled former client? I mean, not everyone can be happy about the results they get here."

Chloe sighed and glanced out the window again. So did Livvy when she caught the blur of motion. Sunny. She was running past the two pregnant women and toward the back of the garden.

"There's a small creek back there," Chloe said, "and it's one of Sunny's favorite spots. I'll give her a few minutes and then go to her, if that's all right."

Those few minutes might get stretched out a bit, depending on Chloe's responses to their questions, but Livvy agreed that Sunny needed to be checked out.

"Possible disgruntled clients?" Ethan prompted Chloe.

She sighed, nodded. "Yes, there are some who aren't happy with the results. Infertility puts a tremendous amount of strain on a couple's relationship and the couple themselves."

Even though it was barely noticeable, Livvy saw a muscle tighten in Ethan's jaw. Maybe Chloe had hit a nerve. Or it could be any mention of fertility issues triggered memories of Isabel.

"Some clients grow tired of waiting and opt out," Chloe explained. "Some decide to end all treatments and try the adoption route. A handful of those might believe they wasted their time and money here."

"We need names," Ethan said.

Chloe sighed again. "I'm afraid you'll have to get a warrant for that. Or try to get one anyway. As you know, privacy of medical records is protected under the law."

They were, and Livvy knew they probably wouldn't get a warrant for a deep dive into the clients' treatments. Still, they might get names.

"This is a murder investigation," Ethan reminded Chloe, and his tone was all cop now. "One of those disgruntled clients could have murdered Zadie. If you're harboring a killer, do you want that on your conscience?"

Ethan was clearly playing hardball with the woman.

But Chloe didn't jump to give in. "I'll speak with our lawyer and get back to you on that. I'm not promising anything," she tacked on as she leaned back against the sofa. "I know who you are, Deputy Oakley. Your wife was here, and she mentioned you were a police officer. I suppose I could count her as one of those not pleased with the services here."

Livvy silently groaned. Chloe was playing hardball, too.

"My wife's not a murder suspect. She's dead," Ethan stated, his voice flat. But Livvy figured he was trying to tamp down a whole lot of emotion.

Chloe flinched but quickly regained her composure. "I'm sorry for your loss. But I brought her up to show you why privacy is important to our clients. You wouldn't want people poring over the details of her visit here."

Ethan was no doubt ready to respond to that, but the sound of footsteps approaching stopped him. They shifted their attention toward the arched entry and saw a man step into the room. It had to be Chloe's brother. They shared the same dark brown eyes, and the shape of his face was like his sister's. And like Chloe, his hair was gray, but it didn't make him look old.

*Formidable.*

That was the first word that popped into Livvy's head. Then, a whispered thought followed. *Familiar.*

But he wasn't. Not really. She didn't know him. At least she didn't remember knowing him.

"They're here about Zadie?" he asked, looking at Chloe. His voice was formidable, too.

Chloe nodded, and she seemed to shrink under her brother's scrutiny. Franklin then slid a glance at Ethan and her. A stony one. "Should we have our lawyers present for this questioning?" he snapped.

"That's up to you," Ethan replied, returning the stony look. "Or we can have this conversation at the police station."

Clearly, that didn't please Franklin, and he looked ready to return verbal fire. But the sound stopped him.

A bloodcurdling scream came from outside.

# Chapter Four

That scream got Ethan moving fast. Livvy, too. She was right behind him when they hurried out of the house and to the side yard.

Considering there was a killer at large, Ethan kept watch around them, but he didn't spot any threat. Only the two pregnant women whom he'd seen earlier from the window. They were now huddled together, crouching behind a bench, and one of them screamed again.

"Stop him!" the other woman shouted. She was pointing toward the backyard. "He killed Sunny."

That got Ethan moving even faster, and he resisted the urge to order Livvy to get down, to take cover. He had to trust her on this. Livvy wouldn't intentionally do anything to harm their baby, and if she saw a threat, then she would take measures to protect herself.

She peeled off from him, going to the pregnant women, and Ethan kept running. His gaze fired all around, and he certainly didn't see a man, but there were plenty of places for someone to hide. However, his attention soon landed on Sunny. She was lying in a crumpled heap on the ground.

"Call an ambulance," Ethan yelled to Livvy, and he raced toward the woman while continuing to keep watch for her attacker.

And she had indeed been attacked.

There was blood on the side and back of her head, and while she was breathing, she wasn't conscious.

"Oh my God," he heard Chloe blurt on a gasp.

Moments later, she and her brother came rushing toward Sunny, both of them dropping down next to the woman. Franklin practically shoved his sister aside though and began checking Sunny's injuries.

"Ambulance and backup are on the way," Livvy let them know.

Good. Now Ethan had to hope that Sunny's injuries weren't life-threatening and that she could soon tell them who'd attacked her. For now, though, he might be able to get that information from the two pregnant women, Hannah Brooks and Leah Parker.

Ethan didn't have to tell Franklin and Chloe to stay with Sunny. Both obviously intended to do just that, and they'd do a better job tending to her than he would since they both had medical training. Still, he'd keep an eye on them.

Because one or both of them could be connected to Zadie's murder.

While there was no evidence to indicate that at the moment, the investigation was in its early stages, and either one of them could have had means and opportunity to kill her. As for motive—well, that might come to light, too.

Ethan went to Livvy, and while continuing to keep watch, he stooped down next to the three women. "Are either of you hurt?" he asked Hannah and Leah, and they both shook their heads.

"Hannah saw a man wearing a ski mask come out from those trees," Livvy explained, pointing to the area dead center of the backyard, where there were more of those pecan and oak trees.

"He ran straight toward Sunny and clubbed her on the head with something," Hannah said, picking up the explanation. She was crying and her breath was gusting, but she seemed determined to get out the account. "I think it was a crowbar. God, he hit her right on the head, and when she fell, he started dragging her toward the trees."

That was awfully bold, or desperate, considering there were two cops inside the house and two potential witnesses on the grounds. But why had this guy taken that kind of risk to get to Sunny?

"Leah started screaming," Hannah went on, "and that must have spooked him because he dropped Sunny and ran away."

So, desperate but not stupid. It would have been next to impossible to drag Sunny into the woods once he'd realized that someone was aware of what he was doing.

"Did you recognize anything about the man?" Livvy asked.

Both women shook their heads, and it was Hannah who added, "He was wearing jeans and black T-shirt."

"What about his build?" Ethan pressed.

More headshakes. "I didn't get a good look at him. Average, I guess," Leah said. "It happened so fast. Seconds. And he kept the mask on. I couldn't even see the color of his hair."

Ethan wanted to ask if it could have possibly been Anthony, but he didn't want to plant that possibility in their heads. It could taint their account of the incident and end up pointing the finger at an innocent man while the real attacker went free.

"Are there security cameras on the exterior of the building?" Ethan called out to Chloe and Franklin.

"No," they answered in unison, and neither took their attention off Sunny.

Too bad about no cameras, and Ethan didn't want to go sprinting into the woods, looking for Sunny's attacker. The guy could double back and come after her again. Livvy would no doubt be able to defend herself and the others, but it was a risk to take. Best to wait for that backup.

And to keep an eye on Chloe and Franklin.

He debated having Livvy go inside with the surrogates, but Ethan couldn't be sure that the attacker hadn't slipped inside. It made more sense to keep everyone where they were.

"Wait here," he muttered to Livvy. "I'm going to keep an eye on Sunny."

Their gazes met, and he thought she might've been surprised that he'd want to do that. But he saw the suspicion in her eyes when she glanced at Chloe and Franklin. So, Livvy had picked up on a bad vibe with them, too.

Ethan rushed back over to Sunny, and he watched as the siblings were having some kind of power battle. Chloe tried to take Sunny's hand, but Franklin shoved her away.

"Go inside and get my medical bag," he snapped to Chloe.

"The attacker could have gone inside," Ethan pointed out. "What's in the bag that would help with this?"

Franklin shot him a glare that practically shouted *Don't you dare question my authority*. But the doctor didn't spell out what medical equipment he had that could indeed help. Sunny was breathing on her own, and the bleeding had slowed considerably. She still wasn't conscious, and that was a huge concern, but Franklin likely wouldn't be able to perform needed tests here. That would have to be done at the hospital.

"Who did this to her?" Chloe asked, her voice and hand trembling.

"Hannah and Leah saw a man in a ski mask," Ethan let them know, and he carefully watched their reactions. "Any idea who that could have been?"

"No," Franklin was quick to snap, but Chloe hesitated.

"Did they get a good look at him?" the woman asked.

Ethan shook his head, not only because it was the truth but also because he didn't want the surrogates to become targets if a killer thought they could ID him.

In the distance, Ethan heard the welcome sound of sirens for both the ambulance and backup. He stayed put, right next to Sunny, until the ambulance came to a stop in front of the house and EMTs barreled out. Right behind them, he saw his fellow deputies Bennie Whitt and Eden Gallagher.

Ethan backed away so the EMTs could get to work. So did Chloe, but Franklin looked ready to stand his ground before he finally stepped back.

Bennie and Eden went straight to Livvy and the surrogates, and Ethan joined them. Eden took one look at Livvy, and she obviously saw how shaken she was because Eden then turned to Ethan.

"Livvy and you should follow the ambulance to the hospital," she insisted, giving an uneasy glance around the grounds. No doubt looking for a would-be killer. "Bennie and I can handle this. Should we be concerned about any of these people being in on the attack?" she added in a whisper.

"Those two," Ethan replied, tipping his head to Chloe and Franklin. "No proof, just a bad gut feeling."

Eden nodded. Like him, she'd been a cop long enough to trust those gut feelings.

Ethan took hold of Livvy's arm to help her get to her feet, and he got her moving toward the cruiser. He held his breath until they were inside. The odds were Sunny's attacker wouldn't fire shots at them—if he'd had a gun, then he likely would have used it on Sunny—but it was best not to take the risk.

He watched as Eden led the surrogates into the house and Bennie talked with Chloe and Franklin. The EMTs did their thing and got Sunny stabilized and onto a stretcher before they started moving her toward the ambulance.

"There's something familiar about Franklin," Livvy muttered.

That got his attention.

"I'm not sure what," she quickly added. She groaned and scrubbed her hand over her face. "It feels as if a memory of him is right there, right on the fringes of my mind. But it could be nothing," she conceded. "I could have maybe seen his picture in the news or on social media. Heck, even if he came into town."

All of that was possible, but Ethan heard the worry in Livvy's voice. And it was for a good reason. Someone had lured them to the scene of Zadie's death, someone who wanted to drag them into this investigation. Maybe to expose Livvy for something that'd happened when she was a kid.

Or to get revenge.

Before he could voice that possibility, his phone rang, and he saw Grace's name pop up on the screen. "Eden just gave me an update," the sheriff said the moment she was on speaker. "Is the injured woman on the way to the hospital yet?"

"The ambulance is about to leave," Ethan let her know.

"Good. I'll have Rory meet the ambulance and stay with

her," she explained, referring to Deputy Rory McClennan. "I'm setting up a search of New Hope, both the house and grounds, and working on a search warrant. I need Livvy and you back here to interview Anthony Carter."

"He's there?" Ethan asked.

"He'll be here any minute," Grace replied, "and he seems eager to cooperate."

Good. Because Ethan was eager to ask the man some hard questions. "Livvy and I are on the way," he assured the sheriff, and they ended the call.

And he glanced at Livvy.

"Don't ask if I'm up to this," she insisted as she drove away from New Hope. "I'm not going to bury my head in the sand. If I'm remembering, then I'll deal with it."

The words sounded right, but he knew what this was costing her. The nightmares and amnesia had eaten away at her. Recalling the truth would no doubt do the same.

Or worse.

Because he couldn't think of a good reason why she'd had trauma memory loss. Or why she'd been found wandering around town with blood on her hands. Or why no one had ever reported her missing.

Yeah. There were some very bad possibilities hidden in those blank spots of her mind.

Livvy pulled to a stop in the parking lot of the police station, and they used the side entrance to head to the bullpen. Ethan immediately spotted Grace at her desk, and she was having what appeared to be a very intense conversation with someone. He also saw the sandy-haired man with the bulky build going through the metal detector.

"Anthony Carter?" Ethan asked him, and he got a quick nod.

Not a friendly one though. Anthony looked intense and

riled. What Ethan didn't see were any signs of grief. Surely he'd heard about Zadie's death, but maybe the man didn't consider that to be terrible news.

When Anthony was finished with the metal detector, he made his way to them. "Sheriff Granger?" he asked, looking at Livvy.

"No. I'm Deputy Walsh, and this is Deputy Oakley," she said.

"Walsh?" Anthony repeated, and he seemed to do some kind of mental double take.

She nodded. "We'll be taking your statement." And as if she hadn't just gone through a morning from hell, she motioned for Anthony to follow them down the hall and into an interview room.

Ethan activated the recording and recited the time, date and those present. "Mr. Carter—"

"Call me Anthony," the man interrupted, taking a seat at the metal table.

"Anthony," Ethan obliged, though he wondered if the cooperation would continue when he added, "I'm going to Mirandize you." That got Anthony's eyes widening, and he looked ready to bolt. "It's standard procedure."

The man didn't look at all sure of that, but he sat quietly while Ethan read him his rights. However, the silence ended the moment Ethan finished.

"Do you think I killed Zadie?" Anthony demanded on a huff.

"Did you?" Livvy asked as Ethan and she sat across from him.

"No," he snapped but didn't volunteer more.

"Where were you last night and early this morning?" Livvy went on, giving him a broad time range since they didn't know exactly when Zadie had been murdered.

"Home in Copper Creek," he said, referring to a small town about ten miles away. "And I was alone so, no, I don't have an alibi. But I didn't kill her." Anthony leaned in. "I'm betting Chloe did though."

"Chloe?" Ethan repeated. "Why would you think that?"

Anthony opened his mouth and appeared to be on the verge of rattling out a quick answer and an equally quick accusation, but then he seemed to throttle back. "I need to start from the beginning."

"Please do," Livvy commented.

But Anthony took a couple of moments and a few deep breaths. "My mother, Ivy Milbrath, was murdered when I was ten years old. Someone ran her off the road and down a steep bluff." He paused again. "She was a surrogate at New Hope."

Ethan felt the slam of surprise and figured Livvy was having a similar reaction. "Go on," he prompted.

"My dad ran out on us when I was a toddler, and Mom didn't have any particular skill set. So, a friend of a friend hooked her up with New Hope, and she had two kids for other couples. Then, something went wrong. I'm not sure what, but even though I was ten, I could tell my mom was scared. Shortly thereafter, she was killed."

Ethan held up a finger to pause Anthony, and he did a quick search on Ivy Milbrath. Sure enough there was a cold-case file on what was classified as a suspicious death.

"Twenty-eight years ago," Ethan muttered.

He heard Livvy's quick intake of breath and knew why. It'd been twenty-eight years since she'd been found in Renegade Canyon.

"After my mom was murdered, I went to live with my aunt, and she adopted me. That's why I have a different surname than my mother," Anthony said when Ethan motioned for him to continue. “Four months ago my adoptive mom died, and I was going through some of my bio mom’s old things that had gotten boxed away. I found a diary.” He took it from his pocket and slid it across the table to them. “Go to the page I’ve dog-eared.”

Ethan did, and the words practically jumped off the page at him. “‘Chloe’s on the warpath again,’” he read aloud. “‘Chloe’s jealous of her lying, cheating husband, and she accused me of sleeping with him. As if. The man is slime. But I don’t think Chloe believed me, and when she’s like this, she’s dangerous as hell. I think I should go to the cops.’”

“She didn’t go to the cops,” Anthony said. “She didn’t get a chance because someone killed her.”

“And you think that someone is Chloe,” Livvy stated.

“I do,” Anthony said with complete assurance, “and after I found that diary, I went to the San Antonio police, but I could tell they weren’t going to do anything. So, I took matters into my hands.”

That wasn’t something a cop wanted to hear. “How?” Ethan demanded.

“I arranged to meet Zadie. I figured she’d know the ins and outs of New Hope. And yes, I started dating her hoping I could get answers about my mother.”

Ethan thought about those lies that Sunny had caught Anthony in. That explained why he’d known about the root cellar and the different color paint.

“Did your mom ever take you to New Hope when you were a kid?” Ethan asked.

“More than that. We lived there during the two surrogate pregnancies.” Anthony paused. “I was worried about Chloe or Franklin recognizing me, but they didn’t.”

Ethan believed that. If they remembered him, they

would have likely said something during the interview. Then again, maybe Chloe and/or Franklin had stayed quiet to find out what Anthony wanted.

"Did you find anything to connect to your mother's death?" Livvy came out and asked.

Anthony cursed under his breath. "No. But I'm sure something is there."

Maybe, and if so, perhaps whatever it was could be found with a warrant. If Grace managed to get one, that is. Getting one for the grounds would be a cinch since Sunny had been attacked outside, but a judge might not be willing to extend the search to inside a medical facility.

"I'm guessing you were very upset when you didn't come up with proof," Ethan commented.

"Of course I was," Anthony snarled. "And then Zadie caught me snooping around in some files and told me to get out."

"Files?" Livvy questioned. "When and where was this?"

"In Chloe's office about a month ago. Zadie was livid and said if I didn't leave right away, she'd tell Chloe, who would probably have me arrested. So, I left and figured I'd have to find another way to get what I was looking for."

"How?" Ethan pressed.

"Well, not by killing Zadie, that's for sure." He muttered more profanity under his breath and shook his head in disgust. "I've been going through my adoptive mother's things, looking for something. Anything," he amended. "She was a therapist, and I remember someone mentioning that she had some patients who were former surrogates at New Hope."

Livvy moved to the edge of her seat. "Your adoptive mom, what's her name?" she asked, and Ethan heard the instant alarm in her voice.

"Dr. Meryl Carter," Anthony said, and he pinned his attention to her. He didn't smile, but his mouth twisted into what seemed to be amusement.

Livvy stood so fast that her chair fell back, clattering onto the floor. "Interview paused," she said for the sake of the recording and added, "I need a minute."

She rushed out of the room, and Ethan was right behind her. "What's wrong?" He couldn't ask fast enough. He led her down the hall and out of earshot from Anthony.

"Dr. Meryl Carter," she repeated, her voice a tangle of raw nerves that matched her expression. "She was my therapist when I was a teenager. And God, Ethan, I told her every detail about the nightmare."

Hell. Ethan had no trouble connecting the dots. Anthony had admitted to going through his adoptive mom's files. So, he knew. Anthony would know exactly how to set up Zadie's murder.

But now the question was why would Anthony have done that?

# *Chapter Five*

Livvy had to fight the panic she felt clawing its way up her throat. It was closing in, smothering her, causing her to feel her control slipping away.

Ethan must have realized what was happening. Of course he did. He'd been her champion and her rescuer for years when they were growing up. Rushing into her room at night to wake her from the horrible dreams. He'd been there, too, when the flashbacks had been so bad they'd brought her to her knees.

Like now.

The mother lode of flashbacks. The dead woman in the tub. Zadie, dead and posed the same way.

Blood on her own six-year-old hands.

Livvy could practically see that blood now. Could smell it. And could feel that fear that she'd experienced as that traumatized child. She'd told every bit of what she remembered to Dr. Carter, and now the therapist's adoptive son had just admitted he'd gone through her files. So, he knew.

God, he knew.

"This way," Ethan insisted, hooking his arm around her and pulling her into the small observation room. He shut the door, whipped out his phone and texted Grace. "I'll ask her if she can get someone else to finish the interview."

Livvy groaned. She hated that she couldn't do her job and was putting this on her boss, but she was too shaken to finish the interview. Too close to the detail. And that kind of closeness could fuel mistakes.

With that reminder, she looked up at Ethan. He was typing away at the text on his phone, but he was certainly close. So close that it both helped and hurt. Livvy felt her nerves start to settle. Ethan could work miracles like that—an instant soother for the flashbacks. But that closeness lit up the fire that always seemed to be simmering between them.

"Grace will handle it," he said when he got a reply to his text. "She'll do the interview herself, and we'll soon have a report on Ivy Milbrath and Chloe's marriage and divorce."

He looked at her then, their gazes colliding, and he must have seen that heat in her eyes. No way to shut it down, and over the years, she had tried. Mercy, had she. Nothing had worked.

Normally, Ethan just turned away or quickly found an excuse to put some distance between them. But he didn't do that now. On a sigh, he pulled her into his arms.

"I can't be weak," she muttered. "I need to face this head-on."

"You are facing it," Ethan assured her. She felt his warm breath brush against her cheek. Almost a kiss. And yes, that calmed her, too.

Along with giving her a tug of that heat.

But unwanted heat was far better than the stomach-twisting panic.

"I'm letting Grace down by walking out of that interview," Livvy insisted, and even though she hated to do it, she stepped out of Ethan's arms. Ready to go back into that room with Anthony.

Ethan stopped her by taking hold of her arm. "Play this out in your head. If Anthony did kill Zadie and he used info from your childhood trauma, then it's best if Grace does the interview. You're too close to this. Hell, I'm also close to it," he admitted. "I've seen you go through the nightmares, and I know what they do to you. If Anthony is toying with that to get back at you, then it's best if we hand over the questioning to someone else."

Ethan was right about this being too personal. The entire investigation was for both of them. And to add to the problem, there were all those blasted blank spots in her memories.

"Maybe I killed Anthony's mother when I was six," Livvy threw out. "I don't remember doing it, so I have no idea what would have prompted me to resort to something like that."

"To *possibly* have resorted to it," Ethan corrected. "When you were six, you were scrawny. A grown woman could have easily fought you off."

She wanted to believe that, but why had she had blood on her? And did that blood have anything to do with Ivy?

"There's also a chance that you were around when Anthony's mother was murdered, and he might believe you can tell him the identity of the killer," Ethan reminded her.

Livvy considered that. And she certainly didn't dismiss it. But it seemed extreme for Anthony to stage Zadie's body to trigger those memories in Livvy to help him bring his mother's killer to justice.

Of course, there was also the possibility that Anthony might not have even been responsible for Zadie's death. Yes, he was a person of interest, but so far, there was no concrete evidence linking him to the crime.

She was mulling that over when their phones both

dinged with an incoming message. "It's the reports on Chloe and Ivy Milbrath," Ethan relayed to her as he opened the file.

Livvy opened her copy, too, and saw the first report was the information on Ivy. As Anthony had said, she had been run off the road and her car had gone over a bluff. The vehicle had then caught fire, destroying a good portion of Ivy's body along with any potential evidence.

Her attention froze on the summary from the medical examiner. It appeared that Ivy had stab wounds, so there was the possibility the woman had been dead before the car crash. If so, then someone could have put her in the vehicle and then pushed it over the bluff.

"Stab wounds," Livvy repeated, and she had to fight the blasted flashbacks again.

"Yeah," Ethan muttered, and he sent off another text. "I want the ME's full report to see if Ivy's wounds could possibly match Zadie's. And I also want to read what the CSIs wrote about all of this." He looked at her again. "Because there's no way you killed Zadie, and you sure as hell couldn't have killed Ivy and staged her death when you were six."

No, but it went back to the possibility that she'd seen or heard something. Maybe something her own mother, father or caregiver had done.

Whoever they were.

Because if Livvy had indeed witnessed one of them murdering Ivy, then it could maybe explain why they hadn't come looking for her. She could have incriminated one of them for murder. And the trauma of her seeing something like that might've been the reason she'd blocked it out of her memories.

"Ivy died just a mile and a half from Renegade Canyon

and only a little over three miles from New Hope," Ethan pointed out. "I guess that makes sense since she had a surrogacy connection to New Hope."

Yes, she did. But had the woman been heading toward New Hope? Or trying to get away from the place? That might be something the ME's or CSIs' reports could tell them.

"Chloe and Franklin will need to be reinterviewed," Ethan said as he continued to read. "And I'm betting Chloe won't like the past being dug up."

Livvy had no doubts about that, and she mentally set aside Ivy's death and moved on to the info in this latest report about Chloe. This one had the basics that Ethan and she already knew about the woman's position at New Hope and the fact that she had no criminal record. But there were some details about her marriage and divorce, and that was what Livvy focused on.

"She married Paul Heller when she was twenty-eight," Livvy read aloud. "Thirty years ago. Paul was a real estate agent at the time of the marriage."

"And he later failed at that," Ethan supplied. "He also failed at the investment business he started…with Chloe's money," he tacked on.

Livvy pulled up the photos of the man that'd been included in the reports, and she studied his face. Not familiar. And she didn't get even a trickle of recognition the way she had with Franklin.

Looks could definitely be deceiving, but Livvy could practically see the cockiness oozing from Paul. And he was drop-dead gorgeous, which meant he probably had attracted other women. That could mesh with what Ivy had written about him in her diary.

"Wow," Livvy went on when she saw the divorce summary. “During the divorce proceedings, Chloe proved infidelity to block Paul from getting any portion of her estate.” Which was sizeable. Well over two million dollars. “No details, though, of anyone she would have named to prove he cheated.”

Ethan made a sound of agreement. “I’ll do some digging on that. We probably can’t get a search warrant for the actual divorce decree, but there could be something about it in Ivy’s diary.”

True, and Grace would either have the diary copied or else take it into evidence since it could point to Anthony’s motive for killing Zadie.

“We’ll need to interview Paul, too,” Livvy commented, and she glanced through the rest of the report to see if there was a current address.

And everything inside her went still.

“Paul’s dead,” she told Ethan, and then she stopped reading and looked up at him. “He died in a car accident the year after Chloe and he divorced.”

Ethan muttered some profanity. “That doesn’t feel like a coincidence.”

No, it didn’t. And Livvy went ahead and pulled up the details that were in the police database. Ethan moved closer to her, shoulder to shoulder, so they could read it together.

Livvy immediately saw that it wasn’t the full report, only a short summary. She also noticed that there weren’t a lot of similarities to Ivy’s fatal car crash. Paul had been killed in downtown San Antonio when his vehicle had smashed into the back of a semi. He had been killed instantly.

“No stab wounds,” Ethan pointed out. “No injuries that weren’t consistent with a traffic accident.” He stopped though when they got to the tox results. "He had a huge dose of muscle relaxers in his system."

He had indeed. But according to the ME, Paul's doctor had prescribed the medication for a back injury. So, maybe Paul had just taken too many and made the mistake of getting behind the wheel. That didn't feel right though, and Ethan must have decided the same thing.

"I'll request the files on both the police investigation and the autopsy," he said, switching away from the report to do just that.

He had barely finished the message when his phone rang, and Livvy saw *County Crime Lab* pop up on his screen.

"Deputy Oakley," Ethan answered with the call on speaker.

"It's Harris," the caller said. No need for him to give his surname, Mendoza, since both Ethan and she knew the lab tech. "I just tried to call the sheriff, but it went to voicemail."

"She's tied up in an interview. How can I help?" Ethan asked.

"I just examined the knife that was sent over as highest priority," Harris explained. "No results on the blood yet. That'll be a while since it's degraded. But there were fingerprints." He paused, and it sounded as if he dragged in a long breath. "The prints were small, almost certainly made by a child."

Livvy felt as if someone had punched her, knocking all of the air out of her. Still, she forced herself to listen to the rest of what the tech had to say.

"We got a match on the prints," Harris said. "And they belong to Deputy Livvy Walsh."

# *Chapter Six*

Ethan set the glass of water on the desk next to Livvy and wished like hell there was more he could do for her.

He wanted to soothe the shock he saw on her face. Wanted to do something to ease that tension in every muscle of her body. He wished he could fix this, but at the moment he couldn't figure out how.

At least this shock and tension were happening in private since Grace had insisted they go to her office and wait for her. Of course, everyone in the bullpen—heck, probably the entire town—would likely soon know about Livvy's prints being on that knife. But for now, Livvy had these quiet moments to settle.

Or rather try to do that.

"Grace will have to suspend me," Livvy muttered. With her elbows on the desk, she covered her face with her hands. "There'll be an investigation, and I'll lose my badge."

Sighing, he dropped down into the chair next to her. "There's already an investigation on the books," he reminded her. "That happened when you were six and Aileen found you. I've read that file. So have you."

And the bottom line was that Aileen and her team of deputies had done a full-scale search to try to find a body or someone wounded, and they'd come up with nothing.

"You won't lose your badge for something that happened when you were a kid," he added.

There was more than a tinge of anger in his voice. He hated that Livvy was beating herself up like this, but he'd be doing the same thing if their situations had been reversed.

"I've been thinking about baby names," Ethan threw out there.

Livvy's hands dropped from her face, and judging from the look in her eyes, he'd surprised her. Of course he had. That was because he rarely talked about the baby or her pregnancy. It was all tied up with the guilt that still ate away at him like acid. But at the moment he thought both Livvy and he could use a change of subject.

"Baby names?" she questioned. No anger in her voice. Just suspicion. She no doubt knew this was a distraction ploy.

But that wasn't all it was.

"In four months we'll be parents," he went on. "And I figure you're thinking about names."

She stared at him. And stared. Then, she nodded. "I've jotted down a few options. I thought when the time was right, I'd run them past you."

What she didn't say was that she had doubts that the time might never be right, but he saw that in her eyes, too. And he hated himself for it. Hated that he'd gotten his best friend pregnant and then basically done an emotional ghosting. This was a major event in their lives, and he'd left her to handle it solo.

Well, no more.

Maybe it was the jolt of seeing this hell Livvy was going through, but he would do a better job of being there for her. And it started now.

"Neither of us have ties to family names," he went on, "but if the baby is a girl, maybe we can go with Mellie."

That got the reaction he'd hoped. Livvy smiled. It was barely there and brief, but the suggestion had obviously pleased her. Mellie Carston was their late foster mother, and along with dozens of other kids, she had given Livvy and him a home and plenty of love.

"Yes," Livvy agreed. "That's the perfect name." And if the baby was a boy, she was sure they could come up with an equally perfect name. "Thank you."

Before he could ask what she was thanking him for, the door opened and Grace stepped in. She immediately volleyed glances at both of them and gave a slight shrug.

"I'm glad I didn't find you in tears," Grace said, aiming the remark at Livvy. She kept her attention on them as she made her way to the chair behind her desk. "How are you holding up?" she added.

"I know you'll have to put me on suspension," Livvy was quick to say.

Grace sighed and leaned back in her chair. "When I was eight, I punched Mike Brennan after he called my mom some ugly names that no kid should have in their vocabulary."

Livvy sighed, too. "That's not the same as my situation."

Grace held up her hand in a *let me finish* gesture. "Mike fell back when I hit him, and he gashed his head on the edge of a locker. He needed a whole bunch of stitches, and I got suspended from school for a week. Now, thirty-something years later, if Mike showed up and insisted that injury had caused some kind of permanent brain damage, should I turn in my badge? Should I stop being sheriff for something I did as a kid nearly three decades ago?"

Ethan could see that Grace's point was getting through

to Livvy. Sort of. "I could have killed someone," she muttered.

"And you could have simply picked up a bloody knife after witnessing something so traumatic that you mentally shut down," Grace was quick to argue. "You could be a witness, not a killer. Which brings me to the knife." She shifted her gaze to Ethan. "No one saw the knife being dropped off at Vernice's. No one," she emphasized.

Ethan studied Grace's expression to see if she had doubts about Vernice's story. Apparently, she did. "You believe Vernice could be involved in this somehow?"

"I'm open to any and all possibilities," Grace replied. "And the questions that come along with those possibilities. Such as, why would someone leave that knife with your former mother-in-law? Was it the killer? Was it someone linked to Livvy's past? If so, why now?" Grace's attention lowered to Livvy's baby bump.

Hell. That got Ethan's mind whirling with some bad thoughts. "Vernice could want Livvy and me in hot water." He mentally took out the *could*. Vernice hated Livvy and him. No doubts about that.

"My prints are on the knife," Livvy pointed out.

Grace nodded. "Yes, they're on a knife with no clear chain of custody. We have no idea where it's been for all these years or whose blood is on the blade. We don't know if your prints were planted on it. The lab is looking into that," she added, swiveling her chair toward Livvy. "All of that is up in the air, especially why someone would involve Vernice in this by leaving her the knife."

Yeah. That was a puzzler all right. And then Ethan recalled something. "Vernice had fertility problems. I remember her sympathizing with Isabel about it."

"Bingo," Grace said. "I just spoke to my mom about

this, and she recalled Vernice going through fertility treatments, and she's almost certain that some of those treatments happened at New Hope."

Ethan cursed before he could stop himself. That was not a connection he'd expected. Or wanted to hear. Because Vernice did indeed have motive for wanting to ruin Livvy.

But murder?

He still couldn't see her going that far.

"Maybe someone else killed Zadie," Grace said, as if reading his thoughts. "And Vernice could have tried to capitalize on it by having the knife come to light."

Livvy shook her head. "But how would Vernice have gotten the knife in the first place?"

"That's what I intend to find out. But you two will have to stay out of that," she insisted. "I'll interview Vernice and try to establish the timing of her treatments at New Hope. Those could coincide with when Livvy appeared here in town."

True, and if so, Vernice might have info that was critical to this investigation.

"Now," Grace continued, steepling her fingers as she rocked back in the chair again. "Do either of you want any downtime—"

"No," Livvy and he blurted out in unison.

It was Livvy who continued: "I don't want to be shut away at home with the images of Zadie's dead body to keep me company."

"Fair enough," Grace concluded. "So, I'll lay out what needs to be done." She paused and gathered her breath. "I had to cut Anthony loose. No grounds to hold him, much less arrest him. But I do have his mom's diary, and I'll have Eden go through that line by line."

Good. Because there might be info in there to blow this

case wide open. "Did we get the warrant to search New Hope?" he asked.

"Nope." Grace muttered some profanity under her breath. "And Chloe and Franklin have made it clear that they won't be volunteering any info about their clients or surrogates."

That wasn't much of a surprise, especially if Chloe or Franklin had something to hide.

"Since we can't get into the files, we talk to the former clients, employees and surrogates," Grace explained. "Rory's coming up with a list now. I'll divvy that up once it's done. For now, though, I'd like the two of you to go to the hospital and try to talk to Sunny."

"She's awake?" Ethan asked, already getting to his feet.

Grace nodded. "I got a text right before I came in here. Of course, her doctor is probably going to frown on her being interviewed by the cops, but this is a murder investigation, so you won't get stonewalled."

No, they wouldn't, and hopefully Sunny would cooperate as well. With her sister dead, though, she might still be in shock.

"And FYI," Grace added as Livvy and he headed for the door, "if you need that downtime, just let me know."

They both assured her they would, knowing that such a request just wasn't going to happen. Livvy was right—better to be out and doing something to solve this case than sitting around and having it weigh them down. Besides, with all the moving parts of this investigation, Grace had to be short-staffed right now.

Livvy and he got in the cruiser and drove the handful of blocks to the hospital. Even though Ethan had plenty on his mind, the reminder of the ultrasound popped into his head. It was scheduled for tomorrow, and it would be done at this very hospital. He wasn't even going to try to convince himself that this was a routine appointment. None of the OB visits were. They were exciting but also carried with them that sickening slam of guilt.

He had to nudge that feeling aside, again, when Livvy pulled to a stop in the spot reserved for Renegade Canyon Sheriff's Office. They both glanced around, checking to make sure there was no sign of trouble. There wasn't, so they went inside.

And soon saw that here was the trouble.

"Thank God you're here," the on-duty nurse, Marilyn Darnell, blurted. She was hunched down behind her desk, and there was a look of raw panic on her face.

"What's wrong?" Ethan couldn't ask fast enough.

"I just heard that a gunman's been spotted," Marilyn said, her voice as tight and tense as her expression.

Hell. What was going on? He didn't have to wait long to find out. His phone rang, and he answered it right away when he saw Grace's name on the screen.

"Livvy and I are here at the hospital," Ethan let the sheriff know, and then they moved behind the reception desk, taking cover in case a shooter came running in.

"I've got a report of an armed man wearing a ski mask," Grace informed them. "Last seen in the patients' wing."

Ethan cursed. Because that was where Sunny was. "Have shots been fired?" he asked.

But Grace's response wasn't necessary because at that moment Ethan heard the too-familiar sound of gunfire. Two back-to-back shots. And yeah, they were in the patients' area.

Grace must have heard the shots as well because she, too, did some cursing, "The security guard on duty is Teddy Mercer," the sheriff explained. "He's just let me know that he's been shot and is pinned down by the nurses' station. According to Teddy, there are other injuries, possible fatalities as well. He didn't sound good, Ethan. And I'm on the way there now," she added as she ended the call.

It wouldn't take Grace and other deputies long to respond, but no way could Ethan just stand by when lives were on the line.

Then, he thought of Livvy.

Of their baby.

"I'll be careful," she insisted, as if she'd known exactly what he had flashed in his mind.

There was the sound of another gunshot, and Ethan knew he didn't have time to debate this with her. They had to do their jobs. They had to act now.

"Find an office and lock yourself in," Ethan instructed the nurse. Better that than her using a desk for cover or running outside and into an escaping gunman.

Livvy and he drew their guns and started moving, and Ethan positioned himself in front of her while they hurried up the hall and toward the back of the hospital to the patients' rooms. It wasn't a huge building by anyone's standards, but it seemed to take a couple of lifetimes for them to reach that area.

They pulled up at the mouth of the corridor and peered around the corner of the wall. Ethan didn't see a single soul on the right, but his stomach dropped to his knees when he saw the security guard, Teddy, slumped against the wall next to the nurses' station. There was a puddle of blood around him, and he wasn't moving. The irony was that medical attention was likely steps away, but no one could safely get to him.

Ethan had to try to settle down his heartbeat drumming in his ears so he could hear what the heck was going on.

There wasn't any more immediate gunfire, but there was someone moving around several rooms up from them. Possibly the shooter. Possibly a patient trying to stay out of the line of fire.

He considering calling out, identifying himself and then demanding the gunman surrender. But that could possibly lead to a hostage situation. In fact, that could already be happening.

"Wait here and cover me," Ethan told Livvy.

Until he added that last part, he could practically feel the argument Livvy was about to dole out. But the truth was that staying put was not only the safe thing for her to do—it meant she could watch his back and maybe stop anyone else, including him, from being shot.

Ethan glanced around himself again, assessing his surroundings. There were five rooms on each side of the corridor in both directions for a total of twenty, and about half the doors were open. It was possible that some of those were empty or that patients had tried to barricade themselves in.

But it was equally possible that the shooter was in one of them.

He eased away from the wall, and keeping his steps as light as possible, Ethan started moving. With rooms on both sides of him, he had to go slow, checking each one before continuing. When he reached the sound of that movement, he stopped and listened.

Footsteps and whispers.

The door was partially open but not wide enough for him to see inside. Gathering his breath, Ethan eased it open with his boot, automatically bringing up his Glock.

And he took aim.

A female nurse and a patient were cowering on the side of the bed. Not Sunny. Nor was the shooter in sight.

*Where is he?* Ethan mouthed.

The women were clearly terrified, but the nurse motioned toward Ethan's left. So, that was where he went. Still keeping that slow pace, he checked the next room. Empty. And he kept moving.

He cursed, though, when he sensed movement behind him and saw that Livvy had stepped out into the hall. Hell. He didn't want her in the middle of this. But Ethan didn't get a chance to make it clear he wanted her behind cover.

That was because of the muffled scream.

It was coming from just one room over, and Ethan hurried there, pulling up by the door frame and peering inside. His stomach dropped when he saw the woman in the corner of the room.

And the ski-masked man behind her.

He had his arm hooked around her neck and a gun pressed to her head.

Again, the woman wasn't Sunny. But Ethan knew her. She was Leslie Stewart, the high school librarian, and he had a vague recollection of someone saying she'd needed an emergency appendectomy.

"Help me," Leslie muttered, and the woman's face was a mask of sheer terror.

The man shifted the gun toward Ethan. And fired. Ethan ducked out of the way barely in time, but the bullet shattered a chunk of the doorframe. He prayed the shot hadn't gone into the room across the hall and injured someone there.

"I'm Deputy Oakley, Renegade Canyon Sheriff's Office," Ethan called out. "Put down your weapon."

He hadn't expected that to work. And it didn't. There

was the sound of more movement, and several moments later, Leslie and her captor appeared in the doorway.

"Come at me and she dies," the man snarled.

Ethan couldn't see his eyes. Heck, nor any part of his face or hair. And he didn't recognize the voice.

So, who was this?

Soon he hoped to get the answer to that, but for now, Ethan was forced to duck into the room across the hall for cover. The gunman took cover, too, by keeping his back pressed to the wall as he dragged Leslie along with him to the next room. Clearly, he was looking for someone, and Ethan decided to test some waters.

"If you're here for Sunny," Ethan called out, volleying quick glances into the hall, "she's been moved."

That stopped the thug in his tracks, and it gave Ethan some critical info. Yeah, the guy was here for Sunny, which meant this was likely connected to Sunny's attack and Zadie's murder. It was possible her killer was right here, just a few yards away from Ethan.

"Where the hell is she?" the gunman snapped.

"In here behind me," Ethan lied without hesitation. He definitely didn't want this SOB checking any of the other rooms since Sunny would be in one of them.

Ethan glanced out in the hall again and saw that the gunman had turned in his direction. His gun was aimed at Ethan, too.

The man still had Leslie in a chokehold, but the woman's gaze met Ethan's. Just for a split second. Enough time for him to motion for her to drop down. It was a risk. Anything they did at this point was. But at least Leslie wasn't in the immediate line of being shot in the head since the gun was no longer pointed at her.

Thankfully, Leslie understood, and she let her legs give

way. The gunman tried to catch her, to pull her back in place as his human shield.

But he must have realized it was too late.

The thug readjusted his aim instead. Ready to shoot Ethan. Before Ethan could fire, though, two shots blasted through the corridor. For a heart-stopping moment, Ethan thought he'd gotten it all wrong, that the thug had indeed managed to shoot Leslie. But she was unharmed and was scrambling away from the man who'd taken her captive.

The man wasn't fine.

Far from it.

Ethan whirled to his right and saw Livvy. She was now in the center of the hall. She was in a classic shooting stance, her Sig Sauer trained right on the thug. And she clearly hadn't missed.

The two shots she'd fired had hit the gunman in the head. And with his eyes already blank and lifeless, he dropped to the floor.

# *Chapter Seven*

Livvy sat next to Ethan in the waiting room of the hospital, waiting for Sunny to be medically cleared so they could talk to her. Whenever that would be. Livvy just hoped she could stay on mental autopilot for a while longer until she could get somewhere quiet and process what'd happened.

For now, though, she had to focus on the job. On the aftermath of what had been a fatal attack. Focus on the fact that Ethan and she hadn't been hurt and their baby was okay. She knew that for a fact since Grace had insisted she have a checkup and an ultrasound. Livvy hadn't minded since she had wanted the exam for her own peace of mind. Added to that, it meant she wouldn't have to keep her ultrasound appointment for tomorrow.

Despite having to fire those shots, they had all come out unscathed. Not the still-unidentified gunman though. And not Teddy either. The security guard was dead, shot and killed in the line of duty, trying to protect the medical staff and patients.

And for the most part Teddy had managed to do just that.

There'd been only one other injury to a nurse who'd been shot in the arm. She was expected to make a full recovery. Ditto for the patients who'd been forced, in some cases, to pull out their own IVs so they could take cover and hide. But all in all, the patients had gotten lucky.

Ethan's phone dinged with a text, and she risked looking at him. Risked because at this point something as simple as eye contact might cause her composure to drop a couple of notches. He no doubt knew that, and he hadn't doled out anything emotional. Just the opposite. He'd been all cop since the shooting, and that gave her some much-needed steadying.

"Hank Stover," he read aloud from the text. "That's the ID that they just got on the dead gunman."

She mentally repeated it a couple of times, testing it to see if it rang any bells. It didn't.

"Aged thirty-nine. A long rap sheet for drugs, assault, robbery. He was from San Antonio," Ethan continued. "Eden is searching for any connection between him, Sunny, Zadie and New Hope."

There would likely be one, but it might not be easy to find, especially if this Hank Stover had been hired to kill Zadie and come after Sunny. If that was the case, who had hired him? Chloe, Franklin or someone else?

And why?

Too bad they wouldn't be able to get the answers from Hank himself, but Livvy knew she'd had no choice but to kill him. If she'd hesitated just a second, he would have ended up shooting Ethan.

"Did you look at the ultrasound?" Ethan asked, the question surprising her.

Livvy turned to him, and yeah, staring at him straight in the eyes packed a wallop. The look alone might have pulled her right in, bringing on the flood of emotion, but then his question sank in.

"No," she answered. "Not really. I just listened to what

the doctor was saying." Especially the part about the baby being all right. "Did you?"

He wasn't so quick to answer, and he finally nodded. "The images were a lot clearer than I'd expected."

"Oh. So, you saw…the sex of the baby." And Livvy wasn't sure how she felt about that.

Nor did she get a chance to think about it because Grace came into the closet-sized waiting room. She handed Ethan a Pepsi and Livvy a small box of milk.

"You got word about the ID of the gunman?" Grace asked, downing some of her own Pepsi.

"Yes," they answered in unison.

"So, you know he was a lowlife son of a bitch before storming in and committing murder." Grace stopped and seemed to be making an attempt to rein in her anger. "Sorry—I just had to do the notification to Teddy's family. Let's just say I have a whole lot of ill will for Hank Stover."

"Same," Livvy agreed, drinking some of the milk. Her stomach was in knots, so she hoped she could keep it down.

"So, here's the deal," Grace went on a moment later. "I've put Sunny in protective custody. This Hank might be a one-off hired gun, but I can't risk her life on it not happening again."

"Sunny must know something if someone sent a killer after her," Ethan spelled out.

Grace nodded. "Or maybe this is all just overkill. Eliminate her in case she knows something that she might have learned from her dead sister." She groaned, drank more Pepsi. "Sunny has to stay the night in the hospital, so Bennie and Rory will cover that, but come tomorrow afternoon, she'll have to go somewhere."

"Not to New Hope," Livvy couldn't say fast enough.

"I can't stop her if she insists on it, and that's where the two of you come in. Sunny has asked to speak to the two of you. I'm not exactly sure what she wants to tell you, but I'm hoping you can work into the conversation that she's potentially in danger and that she needs to stay in protective custody."

"Protective custody with us?" Ethan asked.

Grace lifted her shoulder. "I'm playing around with that idea, but let me back up a bit and spell out what I'm thinking. The two of you have to take twenty-four hours of downtime. Standard procedure after a shooting. Twenty-four hours is about when Sunny will be released."

"Into our custody?" Livvy pressed.

"Yeah. It'll get you off the street. And no, I'm not babying you. It's protocol for a pregnant cop to move to desk duty. Which I know you don't want," Grace added when Livvy opened her mouth. "You could just do the desk duty at home while guarding a woman in potential danger." She stopped again, and concern spread over her face. "How's the security at your houses?"

"Good," Livvy supplied while Ethan said, "Outstanding. I just did a major upgrade."

"Okay, there you go," Grace replied, as if that solved everything.

It didn't. Livvy hadn't been to Ethan's place since the night she'd gotten pregnant. Lots of memories there. Also this chemistry between them. But memories and chemistry would have to take a back seat to keeping Sunny safe.

Grace checked the time again. "All right. Go talk to Sunny. She's been moved to room 116 at the other end of the hall. Let me know what she has to say, and then go home. To his home," she emphasized, tipping her head to Ethan. "Can't beat a major upgrade in security."

No. But Livvy didn't like to lie to herself about such

things. It would be a different kind of hell sharing close quarters with Ethan.

They finished their drinks, tossing the empty containers, before they made their way out of the waiting room and into…chaos. That was the only word for it. The CSIs were in full operational mode, and there were two of their fellow deputies still taking statements.

And then there was the blood.

Teddy's body had already been examined and moved by the county ME team, but the cleanup hadn't started yet, and that blood was a stark reminder of what had happened.

It was easy to find Sunny's door since there was a reserve deputy, Walt Sanchez, standing outside. Walt had obviously known they were coming because after greeting them, he stepped to the side to let them in.

Livvy spotted Sunny right away, not so much lying in the hospital bed but more like cowering in it. She had the cover pulled up to her chin, and she looked ready to jump out of her skin. Livvy couldn't blame the woman. Not once but twice today someone had tried to kill her.

"Deputy Walsh, Deputy Oakley," Sunny said, sitting up just a little. "The sheriff told me what you did. Thank you for saving me." Her mouth trembled. "That man was coming for me. I heard him ask where I was." And the tears began to pool in her eyes.

Livvy decided not to verify any of that. No need to spell it out. Instead, she went with a cop's response. "Did you know the man, Hank Stover?"

"No," Sunny was quick to respond. "The sheriff showed me a picture of him, and I've never seen him before."

So, that added some weight to the theory that he'd been a hired gun.

"Do you think he's the same man who attacked you at New Hope?" Ethan pressed.

"I just don't know. He was wearing a ski mask, and I didn't see his face," she admitted. "But it must have been him, right? I mean, I can't have two people after me, can I? And he must have been the one who murdered my sister."

That trembling of her lips went up a notch, and Livvy so wished she could reassure Sunny that all would be well. But she couldn't. It was better for Sunny to understand that they still had a lot of unanswered questions and that she was still in danger.

"We're looking into that," Livvy settled for saying. "We're looking into a lot of things, and we need your help."

"I'll do anything." This time, the tears spilled down her cheeks. "My sister is dead, and if that man was the one who murdered her, I want to know why."

Ethan nodded and moved closer to the bed. "Had anything unusual been going on with Zadie in the last couple of weeks?"

"You mean something other than her break up with Anthony," Sunny muttered, and then her head whipped up to spear them with her gaze. "Did Anthony hire that gunman?"

"We don't know yet," Livvy admitted. "That's why we need all the info you can give us."

Sunny gave a resigned sigh and used the back of her hand to swipe away the tears. "Zadie had been contacting former surrogates and their families, asking them about any irregularities at New Hope."

That got Livvy's attention, and Ethan and she exchanged a glance. "Irregularities?" Livvy questioned.

"Rumors that Chloe and Franklin would purposely cause certain procedures to fail so the clients would have to pay for repeats. Or end up paying for the most expensive gestational-surrogacy service," Sunny said, her voice a tangle of fear, nerves and grief. "Zadie said she had talked to a couple of women who believe that's what happened to them."

"Do you have these women's names?" Ethan quickly asked.

She shook her head, then shrugged. "I'm not even sure it was true. I've never seen any proof of it anyway."

Livvy thought about that for a moment. "Then, what happened to make Zadie believe such things were going on?"

"Because she said one of the women had called New Hope to complain about repeated procedures, and Zadie has passed along the complaint to Chloe. But when Zadie looked, the woman's entire file was missing."

So, maybe that was Chloe covering her tracks. Or Franklin.

"Did Chloe or Franklin kill my sister?" Sunny came out and asked.

Again, Livvy went with the honest answer. "We don't know. Obviously Anthony is a person of interest, too."

Sunny made a soft sound of agreement. She was pressing her hand to the side of her head now and was clearly in pain. "If any of them killed Zadie, I want them punished. I want you to throw them in jail and never let them out."

"We want the same thing," Ethan assured, and he took out a card from his wallet. "My number is on there. Please call me if you think of anything. And don't speak to Chloe, Franklin or Anthony."

Panic shot through her eyes. "They could get in here—"

"No," Ethan interrupted. "You have a deputy guarding your door, and all visitors will have to be cleared through the sheriff. Once you're released, Deputy Walsh and I will be taking over your protective custody."

That eased some of the panic, and Livvy could see the exhaustion moving in to take its place. "Call us if you need anything," Livvy told her.

Ethan and she said their goodbyes, and they headed out. Not far. Just into the hall so that Livvy could text Grace about what Sunny had said. It was hearsay, so it likely couldn't be used to get that search warrant of New Hope's records, but there was a higher priority now to speak to any former clients. Especially since uncovering those *irregularities* could be the reason Zadie was dead and Sunny was in danger.

It didn't take long, less than a minute, for Grace to respond: Once I have the list of names of clients, I'll start interviewing them. For now, you two go home and stay there until you hear from me. I'll let you know if I need you.

"Home," Ethan repeated under his breath, and Livvy heard the same concerns in his voice that she had in her head.

Still, that didn't stop them from moving toward the exit. They made their way through the hospital and out to the cruiser. Both of them looked around, checking to see if the dead thug's boss or a partner was anywhere around, but Livvy didn't spot anything suspicious.

"We can work on the client list, too," Ethan said. "We can look for mentions on social media and such."

Livvy welcomed the task. Not only did it get her mind off sharing a house with Ethan, but it could also help uncover what the heck was going on.

She drove down Main Street and took the familiar turn toward Ethan's. Like most of the deputies in Renegade

Canyon, he didn't live in town but rather on a small ranch several miles away. In Ethan's case, he'd bought the place about a decade earlier, shortly before Isabel and he had married. So, it'd been their home. A place they'd lived when they had intended on starting and raising a family.

Obviously, that hadn't happened.

And it brought her to something that had been niggling away at her.

Livvy hated that this was going to scratch away at old wounds for Ethan, but she didn't think it was something they could just ignore.

"If Isabel went to New Hope, there should be a medical record," she said after taking a deep breath. "As Isabel's next of kin, you could maybe get access to the file. And no, it might not have any indications of one of those irregularities, but I think it's still worth looking into."

And she was babbling. That might have continued, too, if Ethan hadn't stopped it.

"It's a good angle," he muttered, though it was obvious he was still dreading it. "I have no idea if she even had procedures there. Or if she was put on any meds." He paused, swallowed hard. "By then, Isabel and I weren't really talking about what she was doing."

Yes, Livvy had gotten the gist of that five months ago on the anniversary of Isabel's death. Ethan had been drowning in grief and had admitted that the infertility had put a huge strain on their marriage.

"I'd wanted Isabel to stop the treatments," he added a heartbeat later. "She obviously didn't. But she was keeping all of that secret from me."

Livvy wanted to assure him there was nothing he could have done to stop Isabel. She had been driven to have a child. But there wasn't anything Livvy could say that would help with the guilt he was feeling.

It was the same for her.

Isabel had been her friend, and Livvy hadn't been able to get the woman to see the damage that some of the experimental treatments were doing to her health. And Livvy totally understood that obsession.

"When I turned eighteen, I submitted myself to some questionable practices to try to regain my memory," she admitted. "Three sessions with drugs used in hypnosis. Countless hours of therapy, including some that were considered promising and cutting edge. I soon learned that was code for *this might work and you're a test case*."

"I remember," he said, and there was something in his tone that had her glancing at him. "When you were twenty or so, I drove you back from one of those sessions. I was worried about you," he added a moment later.

Yes. She'd been worried about herself. About the thoughts that had come with the attempts to dredge all of that up. And here they were again. The dredging was happening, and there was nothing she could do to stop it.

Her phone rang, the sound thankfully yanking her out of all of those bad memories, and when Livvy saw Eden's name on the screen, she took the call right away on speaker.

"How are you two holding up?" Eden asked.

No small talk. Eden was their friend and had been a cop as long as Ethan and her, and she knew the sickening tangle of emotions that came with having to kill someone in the line of duty.

"We're managing," Livvy said, and Ethan echoed something similar.

"Good. I almost believe that," she remarked. "I might

have found something," she added after a quick breath. "And FYI, I'm not sure if it'll help or hurt."

Livvy felt the dread wash over her. Still, she insisted, "Tell us what you found."

Eden dragged in another breath. "I've been going through Ivy's diary. Since this spans over several entries, I'll try to summarize, and then I'll send you copies of the pages so you can read them for yourselves."

Good. Livvy wanted to read every word of it. Especially since Ivy had died around the exact time that she had been found in Renegade Canyon. They could be connected, especially considering that Ivy had had stab wounds.

"Let me start with the page that Anthony showed you," Eden went on, "and I quote—'Chloe's jealous of her lying, cheating husband, and she accused me of sleeping with him. As if. The man is slime. But I don't think Chloe believed me, and when she's like this, she's dangerous as hell. I think I should go to the cops.' That all sounds as if Ivy wanted no part of Paul, right?" she asked.

"Yes," Livvy verified, wondering where this was going.

"Well, apparently Ivy didn't always feel that way about Paul," Eden explained. "In the entries from the year before, Ivy admitted to having an affair with him."

"Wow," Ethan grumbled. "That was in the diary?"

"It was. So, I don't know if the part Anthony showed you is fake or if he simply refused to believe it. It's also possible he hadn't read the entire diary before today, though that doesn't feel right."

Livvy agreed. The man was on a mission to find who was responsible for his mother's death, and since Ivy had died when he was ten, the diary was his insight into what might have happened.

"He maybe didn't want to paint his mother in a bad

light," Ethan suggested. "Heck, Anthony might not have even considered that we'd take the diary and examine it."

"True," Eden admitted. "But we do have it…and there's something else. Again, I'm going with a summary here because the info spans over about a dozen entries. About three weeks before Ivy was killed, Paul ended their affair. She was clearly hurt and really angry. Lots of profanity and venom aimed at Paul. And also aimed at the woman he dumped her for."

Ethan and Livvy exchanged another glance. "I'm guessing Paul didn't quit seeing Ivy for his wife?"

"No. Ivy called the woman Anna. No surname given," Eden tacked on. "But Ivy said in a couple of the entries that she intended to get back at Anna and Paul. Remember, all of this would have been days before Ivy was murdered."

Livvy was having no trouble seeing the timeline. And that feeling of dread was growing by leaps and bounds.

"There's more," Eden said. "This one entry where Ivy talks about Anna. I'll read this one to you verbatim." She cleared her throat. "'I talked to Anna's kid, and she said Paul had been coming around to see her mom. Out of the mouths of babes. I guess when you're six years old, you don't think to lie about something like that. Or wonder why someone is asking.'"

"Oh, God," Livvy blurted. She hit the brakes and pulled to the side of the road. "Six. I was six."

"Yeah," Eden verified. "And here's the rest of what Ivy had to say—'That bitch, Anna, and Paul are going to pay, and I'm going to use the kid to help me.'"

# Chapter Eight

Ethan stood at the pasture fence and watched his animals. The geese that he'd inherited when he bought the place and the two Appaloosas he'd purchased four years ago. He'd named them Faith and Tim, after his foster mother's favorite country singers, Faith Hill and Tim McGraw.

Since Faith was in foal, she would soon be adding another member to his small ranch. But neither the geese nor the horses needed any special tending from him. Because of his hours at work, Ethan paid someone to take care of that. But watching them soothed him.

Well, sort of.

Nothing was going to do a decent job of soothing, but at least out here he could take in the crisp November air to help clear his head. And he could give Livvy a little privacy to get settled into her temporary quarters.

After Eden had delivered that bombshell about the woman, Anna, and her six-year-old daughter, Ethan had gotten behind the wheel of the cruiser and driven them here. He hadn't peppered Livvy with questions or speculation. Not when she'd had that stunned look on her face. He had just gotten her to his house and led her to the guest room, where he'd suggested she get some rest.

Like soothing, rest probably wasn't in the cards either,

but maybe Livvy could use this time to mentally process what she'd learned. Of course, then the speculation would kick in. The questions without answers.

Was Livvy Anna's daughter?

Had Ivy actually used the daughter to get back at Paul and Anna?

Hell, did Anna and her daughter even exist?

Basically, that was the account of a dead woman, Ivy, and even that was iffy. It was entirely possible that Anthony had constructed the diary. Ethan didn't know why the man would have done that.

Not yet anyway.

But he was hoping Grace would get to the bottom of it when she brought Anthony back in for questioning. Unfortunately, that wouldn't happen until tomorrow morning. Anthony's lawyer had seen to that by insisting he needed to gather some background info before his client was "grilled" again by the cops.

Grace and some of the deputies were gathering info as well. Anything and everything on Anthony, New Hope itself and former clients, surrogates and employees. So far, that number was already over the one hundred mark and growing. Proof of that was the text from Rory that Ethan had gotten just minutes earlier with several pages of names.

Ethan glanced down now at that text, and he sighed. Time to go back in and get started on some research. Maybe he wouldn't wake Livvy if she had indeed managed an afternoon nap.

But no such luck.

He heard the geese squawking—the feathered security system that alerted him that someone was coming. As usual, they were spot on. He turned toward the house and saw Livvy making her way to him. And he got that punch of heat that he didn't want. His body wasn't interested in listening to his brain about that. His body wanted Livvy.

Yeah, even now.

Even with all the guilt that he felt over sleeping with her and getting her pregnant. And now they had the added stress of this damn investigation. One that threatened to rattle Livvy to the core.

As she got closer, their gazes connected, and while she didn't smile in greeting, at least it didn't look as if she'd been crying. That was something.

"Did you tell everyone to keep me out of the text loop for a while?" she came out and asked.

"I did," he admitted. "Hard to sleep with beeps and rings going off every few seconds."

"Hard to sleep, period." On a heavy sigh, she walked closer, stopping right next to him and shifting her attention to the horses. "Any chance that Faith and I will be having our babies around the same time?"

He liked the change of subject. Not exactly neutral, but maybe talk of horses and babies would help ease the tension he could practically feel thrumming off her body.

"I think Faith's offspring will be a little later than yours. Ours," he corrected, and that was somewhat of a victory for him to be able to say that aloud and not think of only the grief.

Now Livvy did smile just a little. It didn't last, of course.

"Anthony must have thought this Anna had something to do with his mother's murder," she said, voicing what was already on his mind. "And I suspect it's possible that Anthony knew exactly what was in the diary, and he wanted the blame pointed right at me. Maybe punishment by proxy if he thought Anna was my mother and that I was somehow involved in Ivy's death."

Again, that had occurred to Ethan, and if it was true, then it meant Anthony was playing some kind of dangerous game.

"It'd be a needle in a haystack to look for women named Anna who gave birth to a daughter thirty-four years ago," Livvy went on. "But that's what I started doing instead of taking that nap. No luck," she let him know.

She followed that with a soft sound of…well, he didn't know. But the alarm zinged through him when she pressed her hand to her belly.

"Are you all right?" he couldn't ask fast enough.

She nodded. "The baby moved." Livvy took his hand, placing it over the spot. "Wait for it," she instructed.

Ethan did, but he didn't have to wait for his body to tell him that this felt amazing. And intimate. The kind of touching couples did, and Livvy and he weren't together like that.

That thought flew out of his head when he felt the little thump beneath his hand. Yeah, definitely amazing, and he laughed before he could stop himself.

"When did that start?" he asked.

"A few weeks ago. The doctor says that's right on time and that the baby's movements and kicks will get harder."

Definitely amazing to think of all that going on inside her, and this was just the beginning. Five months into something that would change both of their lives forever. Heck, it already had.

"You saw the ultrasound," Livvy reminded him. "So, you know whether this is a boy kick or a girl kick."

Ethan nodded and eased back his hand. "I do. Do you want to know?"

She stayed quiet, obviously considering it, and shook her head. "Now doesn't seem the right time. Not with a murder investigation hanging over us. It should be celebrated. Not one of those gender reveals," Livvy quickly added. "Just…uh…well, something we can savor."

*Savor.* A certain part of his body thought that was a great word. An accurate one that didn't only apply to learning such a vital detail about their baby.

Yeah, being around Livvy wasn't easy.

The images of her flashed through his head. Images of that night when she'd been naked and on the sofa with him. He'd kissed her then. Held her. But mainly it'd been a frantic rush to try to sate the fire that had ignited inside them.

The fire that was still there.

Ethan tried to force himself to turn away from her. It didn't work. Nothing did. He just felt that damn heat consuming him again. Felt that need for her clawing away at him.

"Uh, I could go back inside," she offered, clearly aware of what was going on. Of course she was. Because he could see that same fire in her eyes.

She actually managed to move and was in mid-turn when Ethan slid his arm around her and pulled her to him. He did exactly what he knew he shouldn't do.

He kissed her.

Their lips touched. Barely. Breath to breath. But even that slight touch alerted him that this was about to turn into something much more. Something hot and filled with need that could quickly get out of control.

Did that stop him?

Nope. Ethan just skimmed his hand down her back, and he inched her closer. Then, closer. Until their mouths were no longer just touching. Until this wasn't just some peck of comfort either. This was a full-on kiss that kicked up those flames big time.

He deepened the kiss, angling his mouth to hers. Livvy did her own share of maneuvering and angling as well. She had given into the fire and need as quickly as he had. And that wasn't a good thing. One of them needed to stay in control here, or they'd land in bed again.

But Ethan couldn't stop himself. Couldn't stop this out-of-control need he had for her.

She smelled so good, her scent curling around him. He wanted to start a long, slow kiss so he could taste every inch of her. Then he'd make love to her. For hours. A lofty goal since he was already primed and ready to go.

The need just kept on building, rushing through him along with her taste and the feel of her body against him. In that moment, he'd never wanted anyone as much as he did Livvy.

And that came through in the kiss.

He slid his tongue over her bottom lip, tasting her. Taking in even more of her. His pulse was thundering now, his breath was stalled in his lungs, and every part of him was on fire. Still, somehow he managed to hear something.

The geese.

They were squawking, and Ethan instantly knew they were alerting to a visitor. He cursed himself for having Livvy out in the open like this. For letting his guard down. Then, Ethan did more cursing when he saw the familiar car slam to a stop in front of his house.

Hell, it was Vernice.

His former mother-in-law bolted from her vehicle, and Ethan didn't have to guess if she'd witnessed that kiss. She had. No doubts about that. She looked enraged, and she stormed toward them.

"How can you do this to Isabel?" Vernice shouted.

Ethan sighed. Because not once during that kiss had he thought of his late wife. Part of him considered that progress. But that progress certainly wouldn't please Vernice.

"You're betraying Isabel's memory and the vows you made to her," Vernice continued, and she shifted her venomous attention to Livvy. "And you call yourself her friend. Some friend. You bedded her husband the first chance you got."

The anger coiled through him. Normally, he kept his mouth shut around Vernice and gave her lots of leeway because she'd lost a child. But there was no amount of leeway for her to go after Livvy like this.

"Livvy didn't force me to have sex with her," Ethan snapped.

That stopped Vernice in her tracks, literally. The woman sort of stumbled to a stop. For just a second or two, shock widened her eyes before the fury returned.

"How dare you," Vernice snarled, her tone as menacing as the glare she was aiming at him.

Livvy lifted her hands in a *calm down* gesture, and she was no doubt on the verge of trying to placate Vernice. Ethan realized he didn't want any placating. Yeah, Vernice had lost her daughter, but he'd lost his wife, and while that would stay with him forever, he couldn't climb into Isabel's grave with her.

"How dare you," Ethan fired back. Not with venom, but an icy coldness that he hoped conveyed he wasn't going to let Vernice run roughshod over Livvy. "Are you here for a reason other than just to spew more of your rage?"

Vernice had already opened her mouth, but no sound came out. She just stood there, gaping at him. Good. At least she wasn't ranting. But he figured this was just the calm before the storm.

"I'm here," Vernice finally said, speaking through clenched teeth, "to tell you that I heard Livvy had left the station with you. I thought you might bring her here, to my *daughter's* home, and I wanted you to know that I don't approve. I don't want her in my daughter's bed."

"She's not," Ethan quickly replied. "No one is. Because I got rid of that bed shortly after Isabel died."

Vernice looked as if he'd struck her. But again, it didn't cool that anger, and she flung her pointing finger at Livvy. "She could be a killer. Have you thought of that? A killer in my daughter's house."

He heard Livvy make a small sound—part groan, part gasp. Vernice had hit a nerve. Damn her.

"It's time for you to leave," he told Vernice, and Ethan, too, had to speak through clenched teeth.

But Vernice didn't budge, and her eyes narrowed to slits when she looked at Livvy's badge. "You call yourself a cop," she spat out. "You should be locked away. I know all about those nightmares you have."

Livvy muttered something he didn't catch, and Ethan moved in front of her.

"Isabel told me all about them," Vernice went on. "Nightmares that you have of a dead woman in a bathtub."

"Isabel told you that?" Livvy asked.

Ethan's gaze fired to her, ready to tell her that he hadn't spilled anything about that to Isabel, but she added, "Yes, I did tell her about the nightmares. I didn't think she'd say anything about them to you."

"My daughter and I had no secrets from each other." Vernice hiked up her chin as if that was something to be proud of.

Well, Ethan wasn't proud. That felt like a betrayal for Isabel to have given those sort of details to her mother.

"No secrets," he repeated like the accusation that it was. "Such as knowing she was going to a place like New Hope and not stopping her?"

"How was I supposed to stop her?" Vernice snapped. "She had already made up her mind."

"But you approved of her going," Ethan said.

Vernice flinched like he'd slapped her. Her mouth fell open, and for a heartbeat, she just stared at him, stunned. "No," she muttered. "I—I didn't *approve*. I was trying to be supportive."

She looked away, jaw tightening, and when she spoke again, her voice was lower. Raw. "I thought if I gave her my blessing to go to New Hope, Isabel might come back to me. Whole. Safe." A bitter laugh escaped her. "Fat lot of good that did." Her eyes narrowed. "And if you'd gone with her, if you'd better monitored what she was doing, she'd still be alive. As far as I'm concerned, you're responsible for her death."

That comment didn't surprise Ethan one bit. It was the first time Vernice had out-and-out voiced it, but he had always felt that she blamed him.

And he blamed himself.

But he couldn't let that guilt take over now, not when it was obvious that Vernice wasn't finished returning verbal fire.

"Both of you are killers," she went on, shooting glares at both of them. "Ethan murdered my Isabel, and you probably killed someone when you were a kid. Murdered her and then pretended you didn't remember. Just like you killed the woman you 'found' this morning." She put the word *found* in air quotes. "You're a bad seed, Livvy Walsh—"

"Get the hell out of here, now," Ethan growled. "If you say another word, I'll arrest you for trespassing. Leave and don't come back, Vernice. You're no longer welcome here."

Vernice looked more than ready to argue with him about that, but she must have realized this was a fight she wouldn't win against two cops who she'd thoroughly riled to the core. She turned on her heels, and with her arms pumping and curse words flying from her mouth, she went back to her car.

Ethan didn't wait for Vernice to be out of sight before he pulled Livvy back into his arms. "I'm sorry," he said, brushing a kiss on the top of her head.

"I'm sorry, too," Livvy returned.

When she looked up at him, he didn't see the hurt he'd expected. Just the opposite. She looked like a cop.

"Vernice seemed to know a lot about me, my nightmares and New Hope," Livvy said. "She also connected Zadie's murder to one that may have happened when I was a kid."

"Yeah. I caught all of that." He glanced in the direction of Vernice's car as it sped away. "I think I'd like to find out what else Vernice knows. I'll text Grace to see if she's willing to bring her in for questioning."

"Good idea," Livvy remarked as he took out his phone and sent the text. He got a reply in under a minute and relayed it to Livvy. "Grace will contact her and arrange a meeting."

"I wonder if there are any other connections that Vernice didn't mention," she said as they started toward the house.

He nodded. Livvy and he were on the same page. "Let's do some digging on the computer," he suggested.

And despite the hellish experience they'd been through,

well, pretty much all day, it felt good to aim all those emotions and frustrations into something that might give them insights as to what was going on.

Of course, a lot of those emotions were because of that kiss. That scalding-hot moment they'd shared before Vernice had arrived. No way was his body going to let him forget about that, but his brain was pushing him in the right direction.

Find the killer before this spilled over even more onto Livvy.

They went inside, and Ethan got some milk for Livvy and a Pepsi for himself while she booted up the laptop. Dropping down in the chairs in his breakfast nook, they got started. Livvy pulled up everything in the database on Vernice.

Because Vernice had once been a social worker, there were plenty of background details on her. She was fifty-eight, which he recalled was the same age as Chloe. That probably wasn't relevant, but he kept it in mind anyway.

"Born and raised near Renegade Canyon," Livvy read aloud. "The only time she left was for college at UT Austin."

Ethan was scanning the info when his attention landed on something. Hell. Now, that could be relevant. "Look at the address where she was born and raised."

Livvy leaned in closer and made a sound of surprise. "Coyote Creek Road." She turned to him. "That's near the house where we found Zadie's body."

"A stone's throw away," he muttered, thinking of the area.

There were some houses there that had long since collapsed and been reclaimed by the woods, and Vernice had lived in one of them. He hadn't known that.

"Vernice moved back there after college," Ethan went on as he continued to read. "And when her mom passed away when she was twenty-two, Vernice moved into town. She got married, and a couple of years later, she had Isabel."

"So, Vernice would have still been living in that house when I was six," Livvy remarked.

"Yeah." But that might not be connected either. Still, they could try to find out if it was. "I'm sure Grace or someone is running a check on whoever owns the house where we found Zadie's body, but let's do some looking of our own."

Livvy immediately shifted over from Vernice's background info to the county land records' database. Since they had Vernice's maiden name, Sullivan, they were able to get a quick hit.

"Vernice's family owned the land for nearly fifty years," Livvy read. "And thirty-six years ago when she moved into town, Vernice sold it to a developer, who went belly up."

After that, it'd changed ownership a couple of times and now belonged to yet another developer, who was apparently doing squat with it.

"Now for info on Vernice's neighbor," Livvy said, shifting the search to the other property.

It currently belonged to the same developer, and the house hadn't had a resident in over a decade when the owner had died. Ethan followed the ownership trail, working his way back to twenty-eight years ago, when Livvy would have been six.

"Hell," he said when he saw it.

Livvy cursed, too. Because the owner back then was none other than New Hope.

# *Chapter Nine*

There was blood. So much blood.

Livvy could feel the panic taking over. She needed to run. To escape. To put some distance between the blood and herself. But her legs wouldn't move.

And God, she couldn't breathe.

"It's okay," she heard someone say.

A familiar voice. Familiar words. From Ethan.

Then, there was something else familiar. His arms were around her, warm and strong, and he had pulled her to him.

That jolted her awake, yanking her out of the nightmare. Again. It was the same dream but worse. So much worse. Because she'd been the one dead in the bathtub. It was her face. Her lifeless eyes.

Her blood.

"It's okay," Ethan repeated, and he eased back enough to meet her gaze. "You're all right now."

His voice soothed her. His eyes. Everything about him worked its magic, and she felt the icy chill leave her bones.

She wouldn't dare tell him about the details of what she'd just dreamed. No need to put those images in his head, especially since he was already worried about the baby and her.

Livvy looked down at the parts of their bodies that

were still touching. Her breasts were against his chest. She was braless and wearing the loose night tee that she had picked up from her place before coming here. But no sleep clothes for Ethan. He was dressed in his usual jeans and shirt. Ready for work.

"You were awake," she muttered, thankful that her nightmare hadn't gotten him out of bed.

He nodded. "It's nearly eight."

Sweet heaven. She never slept that late, and her attention fired to her phone on the nightstand to verify the time. Yes, it was 7:55. By now she was usually at work or on her way in. But Grace had told them to stay put until they heard otherwise from her, so Livvy hadn't set her usual alarm.

"You should have gotten me up," she said, moving back from him and tossing off the cover. Not the best idea she'd ever had because the sleep tee had ridden up, showing her panties and baby bump.

And Ethan noticed all right.

She saw the mix of emotions swirl in his eyes: The heat and the love for their child. Some discomfort, too, since this had to remind him of the night they had sex and she'd gotten pregnant.

Livvy quickly wrestled with the tee to shove it down, and she got up from the bed. "Have you gotten any updates on the case?" she asked. She'd showered right before bed, so she headed straight into the en suite bathroom to change into the clothes she'd left in there.

"A few," he replied, and she heard the dread in his voice. "None good though. We still haven't been able to get a search warrant for the records or inside New Hope."

Livvy made a sound of frustration even though she'd expected it. Yes, Zadie's body had been found at the house that had once belonged to New Hope, but they hadn't owned the property in over twenty-five years. Which meant New Hope's connection to it was all circumstantial.

"No hits on it yet, but Eden's got a working list of former clients, surrogates and employees at New Hope," he went on, "and she's divvied it up among all the deputies and reserve help. She emailed us our share about thirty minutes ago."

Good. They could get started on that right away. And maybe they'd get one of those hits. All it took was one to blow this investigation wide open.

"The CSIs have processed both the murder scene and the grounds of New Hope and haven't turned up much." Ethan continued with the updates. "They did find some motorcycle tire tracks on a trail behind New Hope, but Hank Stover didn't own a motorcycle."

Livvy considered that a moment. "Are you thinking the tracks were made by someone else?" Because their working theory was that Hank had attacked Sunny and then tried to murder her in the hospital.

"It's possible. We might be after several hired thugs," he said, spelling out what she knew they had to consider.

She finished changing into her jeans, top and boots and came back out to find him sitting on the foot of the bed. Their gazes instantly connected, and yeah, there was the heat. The worry, too.

"What's wrong?" she couldn't ask fast enough.

He took several moments to respond. "I looked back through all of Isabel's medical records that I have here."

Oh, heck. "I'm sorry. That had to be hard for you."

"It was," he admitted. "She kept a spreadsheet of appointments, health-care providers and treatments. And there were some more things in there that she hadn't told me about. Some herbal experimental stuff."

Since it'd been one of those experimental things that'd ultimately killed Isabel, that had to have struck a nerve or two.

Livvy went to him. She sank down on the bed next to him and took his hand in hers. It was a risk. When it came to Ethan and her, touching and intense emotions didn't always lead to good decisions. But she wanted to comfort him as he'd done to her when he'd woken her from this latest nightmare.

"What wasn't in the file was anything from New Hope," he went on. "And I know she went there at least once. Since I doubt Vernice will spill any details about that, I want to go to the source. I want to speak with Chloe and Franklin and demand to see Isabel's record."

No need for her to point out that the record could have been destroyed. Or that Chloe and Franklin could simply refuse to hand it over without a whole lot of legal wrangling—and that could give them time to remove anything that might be incriminating or questionable. Still, Livvy understood why Ethan needed to do this, and she wanted to help with it.

"I'll go with you," she said, and it wasn't a suggestion. She would be with him on this.

He nodded, muttered a thanks under his breath. "I texted Grace and told her what I plan on doing, and she gave a reluctant thumbs-up." Ethan checked the time. "I'd like to leave after you've had some breakfast."

Livvy was all for that, and even though she wasn't hungry, she had made a habit of eating something healthy each morning for the sake of the baby. Ethan had obviously considered that, too, because when they went into his kitchen, she saw the breakfast tacos in the cast-iron skillet on the stove. He dished her up one, added a glass of milk and took a bowl of fresh, cut-up fruit from the fridge. Obviously he'd made good use of the time he'd been awake.

"Thanks," she muttered, sitting in the breakfast nook. The taco was still warm and delicious.

Ethan took a bite of one, too, and he moved the laptop onto the table so they could both see the screen. "I've only researched one name on the list that Eden sent," he explained, pulling up the email. "Chrissie Anne Waterton."

*Anne.* That jumped right out at her, and Livvy stopped in mid-bite of a peach slice.

"I don't think this is the woman mentioned in Ivy's diary," Ethan was quick to assure her.

That eased some of the sudden tightness in her chest, but Livvy still fixed her attention on the name and the handful of details that someone—Ethan, no doubt—had added there.

"There's no record of her ever having a daughter," he explained. "Only two sons who are now in their early twenties. She was a surrogate at New Hope about thirteen years ago."

So, the timing didn't match either. Still, she might be able to tell them something. "Will we talk to her?"

"Eden and Grace will do the interviews once the backgrounds have been complete. Most will happen over the phone. But for any with possible red flags, Grace wants to visit them in person."

That made sense, and Grace might be able to tell if the person was trying to hide something.

"How many names do we have on our share of the list?" she asked and then continued eating her breakfast.

"Eighteen, and it's a mix of clients, staff and surrogates."

"Eighteen," she repeated, realizing that the list had to

be huge since it would have been divided among about a dozen people. And more names would likely be added as info came to light in the interviews.

"None of the other women on our list is named Anne," he told her. "But Eden said she has a couple who are high priority for her."

Yes, priority because this Anne could be connected to Livvy. "I've thought about who my mother might be," she admitted. "And considering the nightmare, I have to believe something…bad happened to her. If that's her in the dreams, that is."

He stayed quiet a moment. "Have you thought about working with the police sketch artist to recreate the face, and then we could try to match it to someone in the missing persons database?"

Livvy had thought about that. And had dismissed it because it'd seemed too terrifying to try to voice all the details. But not knowing was terrifying as well.

"I can do that," she managed to say though the muscles in her throat had gone tight. Before she lost her nerve, she texted Grace to approve it. "I'd need you there with me for that."

"I will be," he assured her, and as if it were the most natural thing in the world, he brushed a kiss on her cheek.

She hadn't needed that kiss, this moment to know just how important Ethan was to her. Steady as a rock. Her best friend.

And she was falling in love with him.

Oh, she had fought that, hard, because with their horrible pasts, their kind of friendship was a lifesaver. Still, she couldn't stop these feeling. The lust mixed with the love. And Livvy was afraid it was going to lead to a broken heart. Because Ethan might never get over Isabel's death. He might never be able to love another woman.

Yep, a broken heart was in the cards for her.

Her phone rang, jolting her out of her thoughts, and Livvy became instantly alarmed when she saw that it was someone from the hospital. "Deputy Walsh," she couldn't answer fast enough.

"It's me, Sunny," the caller said.

"Are you all right?" Livvy asked, putting the call on speaker.

"Uh, no. I mean, yes, I'm safe. The deputy is still guarding my door, and no one has tried to get in." She muttered something Livvy didn't catch. "Sorry—I'm rambling. I remembered something that my sister said, and I'm not sure if it's important, but..." Her words trailed off.

"What did you remember?" Livvy pressed.

"It could have been a joke," Sunny blurted. "But it didn't feel like one. Zadie and I were talking about Franklin. Sometimes he can have that *holier than thou* attitude. Know what I mean?"

Livvy did know and made a sound of agreement, hoping that Sunny would continue and get to the point.

"Anyway, Zadie said she wouldn't be surprised if Franklin had fathered some of the babies with the surrogates."

She certainly hadn't been expecting that. Judging from his expression, neither had Ethan.

"Sometimes when the husbands are sterile or incapable of fathering a child," Sunny added, "donor sperm is used. But Zadie must have seen something in the records because she said maybe Franklin skipped the donors and used his own. I don't know if it's true," she quickly added. "And I have no idea if it's important, but I didn't want to keep it to myself if it could help. Will it help?" she asked after a short pause.

"Maybe. We'll definitely look into it," Livvy assured her. "Do you recall Zadie mentioning if she actually looked at any of the records or talked to anyone else about this?"

"Sorry, no. To be honest, I didn't understand why Zadie even said something like that. I mean, I know she didn't care much for Franklin, so it could have been something just off the cuff, with no proof whatsoever to back it up."

The proof could be in the children who'd been born via surrogates. But Livvy didn't see how they were going to get that kind of DNA data. Still, it was something they could perhaps try to verify with the surrogates themselves during the interviews.

"Thank you for this, Sunny," Livvy told her. "Has the doctor told you when you'll be released from the hospital?"

"Maybe this afternoon, but my blood pressure's a little high, so they might keep me an extra day. I don't mind staying here," she added in a mutter. "I, uh, know I've already told you that I don't want to go back to New Hope. I haven't changed my mind about that."

"I understand," Livvy assured her. "And when you are released, we have a safe place for you to go."

"Good," Sunny said, the word tumbling out with a stream of breath. "Thank you, Deputy Walsh."

Livvy ended the call and looked at Ethan. "Sounds like a motive for murder if Zadie truly did uncover that about Franklin."

"It does. As Sunny said though, Franklin might not have even fathered those kids. And if he did, he possibly had permission from the clients. But if it was all done hush-hush, then that could indeed be motive."

Yes, that could trigger some charges, but more than that,

this could turn out to be a scandal. Something that spread on the news media and ended up ruining New Hope's reputation.

Which gave Chloe motive for murder, too.

Even if Chloe had approved of what her brother might have done, she seemed devoted to New Hope, and she might not want anything to put a stain on it.

But murder?

Maybe. That could be particularly true if the woman had already killed someone before. Livvy thought of Ivy. Of what Anthony had said. And if that was the truth, then Chloe was more than capable of ending a life.

Ethan minimized the list from Eden and used the laptop to do an internet search for mentions of both Hank Stover and Franklin. He groaned when there were no hits, and then he widened the search to include New Hope and Chloe.

"Still nothing," he grumbled.

"Try the names we got from Eden," Livvy suggested.

"Good idea." He copied and pasted the names into the search, and this time, they got something.

"Sherry Elmore," they read in unison. "She's Hank's half sister."

Yes, that was a connection all right. But did it mean anything?

Ethan shifted the search back to police background database, and he pulled up what they had on Sherry. She had a record for DUI, arrested eleven years earlier, and while she hadn't served any time, it was enough to provide them with plenty of info collected while she was in custody. Including her place of employment at the time of the arrest.

New Hope, where she'd been employed as a housekeeper for nearly thirty years.

A position she'd kept until six weeks ago.

"It doesn't prove anything," Ethan admitted. "But we can show Hank's picture to Chloe and Franklin and see how they react."

True, and while it might come to nothing, it felt like *something* to Livvy. Perhaps hitting Chloe and Franklin with this info would rattle them.

"Let's go to New Hope," she said, standing. "You can maybe continue to dig on Sherry while I drive."

Ethan was quick to agree. "I'll message Grace first to bring her up to speed, and then I'll try to call Sherry and speak to her."

He fired off the text to Grace as soon as they were in the cruiser, and she sent a reply within seconds. "She gave the okay for me to contact Sherry. Oh, and Grace said to let you know that you have an appointment with the sketch artist at noon today."

Noon. Still hours away. But she'd need to do some steeling up for that. Still, Livvy was glad it had been arranged.

She kept watch around them as she drove, but from the corner of her eye, she saw Ethan accessing Sherry's phone number from the background. Considering it'd been so many years since her arrest, Livvy knew it was possible that the woman's contact information had changed, so it was a nice surprise when someone answered on the second ring.

"Sherry Elmore?" Ethan asked.

"Yeah," she verified in a snap. "What do you want? If this is about my good-for-nothing half brother, then I got nothing to say to you."

She definitely didn't sound very friendly, but at least

she knew about Hank's death. That meant this wouldn't turn into a notification.

"I'm Deputy Ethan Oakley, and I'm with my partner, Deputy Livvy Walsh, from the Renegade Canyon Sheriff's Office. I understand you used to work at New Hope," he said, obviously steering clear of mentioning Hank for now.

"Yeah, so what?" she barked out.

"We're just doing some backgrounds on New Hope and the staff, and I wondered about your experience working there."

Sherry huffed a humorous laugh. "Well, it wasn't a picnic, that's for sure."

"Could you share any details about that?" Ethan pressed.

"Chloe and Franklin treat their employees like crap. Asking us to do overtime but not paying us for it. Searching us to make sure we weren't taking pictures of clients or recording their conversation."

Livvy glanced at Ethan to see his reaction. Like her, he was no doubt wondering why Chloe and Franklin had insisted on such tight security measures.

"Still you worked at New Hope a long time," Ethan pointed out.

"Yeah, I did. The money was good, and I didn't exactly have a lot of people offering me jobs. And I woulda stayed on had Chloe not fired me."

"Why did she fire you?" he asked.

Sherry cursed. "It started with Chloe yelling at me because I walked in on her having an argument with Zadie. God rest her soul," she added in a murmur. "Chloe said if I repeated a word of anything I'd heard, she'd fire me on the spot and give me bad job references."

"Did you hear what they said?" Ethan asked.

"Nope. But apparently Chloe didn't believe that because she ended up firing me anyway. We have to sign this nondisclosure agreement to get hired there, and Chloe reminded me if I told anyone anything about the goings on at New Hope, then she'd sue me."

That was something they would definitely ask Chloe about, but they'd have to do it in a way that protected Sherry, to make sure Chloe wouldn't be able to sue the woman.

"Did Hank ever visit you at New Hope?" Ethan continued a moment later.

Sherry groaned. "I said I didn't want to talk about him—"

"It's important," Ethan interrupted. "Please. I just need to know if he was ever there."

Silence for a long time. "Yeah. I didn't live at New Hope like a lot of the other staff, so once or twice Hank dropped me off at work when my car was in the shop. And yeah, he did that recently. Now you're thinking Hank saw Zadie and got obsessed with her or something."

Ethan jumped right on that. "Could that have happened?"

"Maybe," she conceded. "Yes," Sherry amended several moments later. "Hank was an arrogant SOB who treated women like dirt. If he put the moves on Zadie and she resisted him, he could have killed her."

Ethan frowned. "Any reason you didn't tell the cops that before now?"

"Yeah, because I haven't had time. I just got off the night shift at the cleaning service where I work. Also, nobody's asked me about him. I only heard about Hank's death about an hour ago because I'm not Hank's next of kin," she added. "Our worthless father has that privilege. He's the one who messaged me with the news."

Now that Grace knew about Sherry and the link to New Hope, she would almost certainly want to do an in-person interview with the woman.

"Is that it?" Sherry snarled. "Because I gotta go."

She didn't wait for Ethan's response but instead ended the call. Ethan texted Grace to give her the update just as Livvy pulled to a stop in front of New Hope. The minute or so that it took him to do that gave Livvy some time to think and process everything that Sherry had just told him.

And now she had to wonder if Hank had acted alone.

Maybe he had become obsessed with Zadie, and since Sunny and Zadie were identical twins, that could explain why one was dead and the other had been attacked.

But while that theory worked, it didn't feel right to Livvy.

Apparently, it didn't feel right to Ethan either. "Hank could have met Chloe or Franklin on one of the visits here to New Hope," he said the moment he'd fired off the text to Grace.

"Yes," she agreed. And that was yet something else they could bring up to Chloe and her brother.

They got out of the cruiser, but before they even rang the bell, a woman in a housekeeper's uniform opened the door. Livvy recognized her from the photos they'd gotten of the current employees, and this was Veronica Baskar.

"I saw you drive up," the woman said, stepping back for them to enter. "Are Dr. Franklin and Chloe expecting you?"

"They'll need to talk to us," Livvy settled for saying.

A sliver of dread went through Veronica's eyes. "I'll let them know you're here. You can wait in the parlor."

Since they knew the way, Livvy and Ethan headed there while Veronica went toward the stairs. They had only made it a few steps when Livvy heard something she definitely hadn't wanted to hear.

A gunshot blasted through the house.

# *Chapter Ten*

Veronica shrieked, and the woman did an about-face, running toward them. Ethan had no doubts that what he'd just heard was a gun going off, and he took hold of Veronica's arm. So did Livvy, and they pulled her into the parlor and behind the wall.

Both Livvy and he drew their guns.

Waiting and listening.

The shot had definitely come from inside the house, but he hadn't been able to pinpoint it. He didn't want either of them to go charging through the place when they could be gunned down. Still, they couldn't stay put either.

Not when someone's life might've been at stake.

Livvy took out her phone, and he heard her call dispatch to report a shot being fired. Good. It meant backup would soon be on the way. As far as Ethan was concerned, it couldn't come fast enough.

Because they might be inside with a killer.

"What was that?" someone shouted. Not Chloe but a woman, and Ethan glanced at Veronica since she would likely know who it was.

She did. "That's Hannah Brooks."

One of the surrogates, he recalled. He'd seen her in the garden shortly before that attack on Sunny.

"Stay put," he told Livvy and Veronica.

With Livvy muttering for him to be careful, he went out into the foyer and saw the surrogate rushing toward him. "In here," Ethan told her, leading her into the parlor. "Did you see what happened? Do you know who fired the shot?"

Hannah's eyes were wide, and her breath was gusting as she frantically shook her head. "Is it someone after Sunny? Because she's not here."

Hell. He'd hoped Hannah might be able to give them some insight as to what was going on. "Could you tell where the shot came from?" he asked.

But before Hannah could answer, there was another gunshot. Then, another. The third bullet ripped through the wall of the parlor too damn close to where Livvy and Veronica were standing.

"Oh, God. Leah and Charlotte are in the kitchen," Hannah blurted.

Leah was the other surrogate he'd seen, and Charlotte was a client. And Ethan soon heard them or maybe someone else. There were definitely some shrieks coming from the back of the house. That was probably where the kitchen was located.

"Charlotte and Leah, get down," he shouted. "Everyone get down," he added in an even louder voice so that anyone upstairs might be able to hear him as well.

Thankfully, Hannah and Veronica instantly complied. Even Livvy ducked down some. Not enough though, and Ethan cursed himself for her once again being in the path of danger. Which meant their baby was in danger, too.

And not just theirs but the babies the surrogates were carrying.

"Is anyone hurt?" Ethan called out a heartbeat later.

"No," several women answered in unison. One of them

might have been Chloe, but he couldn't be sure. What he was certain of was that Franklin hadn't responded. He hadn't heard a male voice.

"Who else is in the house?" he asked Hannah.

She shook her head again, and it took her a couple of seconds to respond. "Chloe and Franklin. And Sienna."

Ethan recalled that name, too. She was a client, and Leah was carrying her child. "What about Sienna's husband?"

"He's not here. Still away on business. And I haven't seen Sienna this morning." Hannah stopped talking and screamed when there was another shot.

"All right," Ethan muttered, pulling his thoughts together. He met Livvy eye to eye. "I'm going to the kitchen to make sure everyone there is safe. Just wait here. I won't be long."

She didn't repeat her *Be careful*, but he could see it in her eyes. Could see the fear, too. It was always terrifying to be caught up in gunfire. It was worse, though, when they had so many other lives at stake.

Another shot blasted into the wall of the parlor, and this time, Ethan had a better idea of where it'd come from—on the other side of the house where he thought there were offices and treatment areas. He wished now that he'd actually studied the layout of the place rather than just glancing at it in the background notes.

He gave Livvy one last look that he hoped conveyed that he didn't want her to take any unnecessary risks. It was just a glance, but a whole lot of things passed between them. They'd both be careful.

And hopefully that would be enough.

Staying low and keeping his gun ready, Ethan slipped out of the parlor. He kept his footsteps as light as possible so he could hear if anyone was approaching. He definitely didn't want to be ambushed or, worse, have the shooter storm into the parlor and start firing.

He threaded his way through the living and dining rooms and into the massive kitchen that spanned the entire width of the house. His stomach dropped when he didn't see the women, but he heard some gusting breaths and whirled around to spot them.

Charlotte and Leah were huddled together on the floor next to the fridge. Both of them were holding huge knives. Good for them. Though knives wouldn't do much good against a gun.

"You're okay?" he verified in a whisper.

The women nodded and continued to cling to each other. "Who's shooting?" Charlotte asked.

"Don't know yet. Have you seen Chloe or Franklin?" he asked.

"No," they replied.

It was Charlotte who continued, "And the other woman who was here left about ten minutes ago."

Ethan's forehead bunched up. "What other woman? A client?"

"I don't think so," she replied. "She was older, maybe in her mid-fifties."

"She came to see Chloe, and I heard her say her name," Leah provided. "Vernice something."

Hell. What was Vernice doing here? Ethan very much wanted the answer to that, but for now, he had a more immediate problem on his hands. He needed to keep these two as safe as possible while he went to check on Chloe and Franklin.

Of course, one of them could be the shooter. And if

so, he'd have to stop them before someone else got hurt or killed.

Ethan hurried to the pantry and threw open the door. It wasn't as large as he'd expected, but he shoved aside some boxes of supplies and motioned for the women to get in.

"Wait in here and stay quiet," he told them. "Backup is on the way."

That news didn't actually soothe the women, but they both scurried into the pantry. Ethan shut the door and hoped it was enough protection for them. It was safer than moving them to the parlor since that was where several bullets had landed.

Ethan hurried back into the parlor, still listening for any other sounds. There were no more gunshots, but he wasn't hearing Chloe, Franklin or the other client, Sienna, either.

"Charlotte and Leah are okay," he told the others and then looked at Livvy. "Vernice was here earlier."

She was clearly just as shocked by that info as Ethan had been. "What was she doing here?"

"Don't know," Ethan replied just as Veronica added, "She didn't stay long and left before you got here."

Maybe his former mother-in-law had left. But it occurred to him that Vernice could be the one who'd fired the shots. He wasn't sure why she would do something like that, but given as much as she loathed Livvy and him, Vernice might have used their visit as an attempt to kill them.

But how would Vernice have known they'd come here? Maybe she had his house staked out, waiting for her chance to get to them.

And that had Ethan debating what to do.

If Vernice was still in the house and if she had killing on her mind, she would almost certainly have Livvy as her primary target. And him. It sickened Ethan to think the woman might do something like that, but he had to at least consider the possibility. But unless she'd had a total break, Vernice would have no reason to hurt any of the surrogates.

"Go to the kitchen," he told Veronica and Hannah. "Take cover in the pantry with Charlotte and Leah. Don't come out until we come get you."

Whenever that would be. Once backup arrived, the entire place would have to be searched.

The women seemed more than eager to do as Ethan had said, and he couldn't blame them. Especially when there was another shot. This one didn't tear through the parlor wall, but Ethan didn't want them to wait around for that to happen. Even if they weren't the intended targets, a bullet could end up killing them.

"Stay low and move fast," he instructed the women, and Livvy and he hurried with them to the kitchen.

Once they were inside the pantry, he shifted his attention back to Livvy. "Please stay behind me," he muttered.

She didn't argue, but he saw the worry in her eyes. "Just be careful," she whispered.

"You, too," he insisted.

And they started toward the other side of the house, where he was pretty sure those gunshots had been fired. He didn't call out to Chloe, Franklin or Sienna. No need to give the shooter their location.

They made their way across the foyer, ducking behind a desk for a moment and listening. There were no sounds other than their quick breaths so they kept moving into the corridors on the west side of the house.

He'd been right about the treatment rooms being here. Two of them. The doors were open, and one resembled the kind of exam area in a doctor's office, complete with adjustable table. The other was more of a surgical suite.

Since there was a lot of equipment in each room, Livvy and he had to check them both out in case the shooter was hiding. Or Sienna, who could be terrified or hurt. But after a thorough search, they didn't find anyone.

In the distance, he heard the sound of sirens. Good. Backup was nearly here, and while he kept watch around them, he took out his phone and texted Grace to let her know their location in the house. Ethan added for backup to approach with caution, and he also mentioned the whereabouts of the women in the pantry.

"They're less than two minutes out," he whispered to Livvy once he'd finished the text.

That didn't put a whole lot of relief on her face, and he knew why. They still didn't know where the shooter was. Or any potential victims.

With that mental reminder, Ethan got moving again. With Livvy right behind him, they went back into the corridor and saw the three other rooms here. Unlike the first two, the doors were shut. And he debated just waiting for backup.

"Someone could be bleeding out," Livvy reminded him.

Her voice was barely audible. Still, he heard her loud and clear and she was right, so they continued to move.

When they reached the first door, they moved to each side of it, and Ethan reached over with his left hand to throw it open. It was a supply room, with everything neatly arranged on shelves. Plenty of stuff, but no one was inside.

They moved to the next room. According to the nameplate attached to the wall, it was Chloe's office. As they'd done with the supply room, Livvy and he moved to the sides of the door, and he was the one to open it.

Hell.

There was nothing neatly organized in here. Folders were scattered over the desk and floor. A chair was lying on its side. And there was a spilled and broken cup of what appeared to be coffee by the window.

What the heck had happened here?

Maybe some kind of attempted robbery? But if so, where was Chloe?

*Bathroom*, Livvy mouthed, tipping her head to the slightly ajar door behind the desk.

They made their way there, and Ethan checked for the scent of a recently fired gun. Nothing. No blood either. That was a good sign. But what wasn't good was the bathroom was empty. No Chloe. Definitely no gunman.

Maybe someone had taken her?

And he thought of Anthony, of the rage the man felt for Chloe. He blamed Livvy and her for his mother's death. So, maybe Anthony had come here to find proof of Chloe's guilt and then things had gone to hell in a handbasket.

His phone vibrated with a text. "From Rory," he told Livvy. "He and Bennie are in the house. They're checking on the women and will start a room-to-room search."

That search would need to include all three floors since it was possible the shooter had slipped up the stairs. Of course, he or she could also be long gone by now. That last shot had been fired well over five minutes ago. Plenty of time to climb out a window and just run.

They moved to the final room, but as they approached, Ethan saw the stairs that were tucked away across from it. The steps led to the second floor, but no one was on them. However, he could hear...something. Maybe someone muttering.

He moved closer, staying in front of Livvy but well

aware that might not be the safest thing. In fact, nothing qualified as safe right now. They could be attacked from behind or from whoever was making that sound. Because he was certain now that it was someone mumbling.

Ethan went up two steps, and he caught movement farther up the stairs. Readying his gun, he pivoted, taking aim. And he saw a woman he recognized from her picture.

Sienna Carrington.

She was cowering behind the banister, crying. She also wasn't alone. Ethan kept his gun aimed when he saw Franklin squatting behind her.

At first, he couldn't tell if Franklin was using Sienna as a human shield or if he was holding her at gunpoint. "Show your hands," Ethan ordered.

They did. Both Franklin and Sienna were trembling, but they lifted their hands into the air. Both sets were empty. But that didn't mean there wasn't a gun nearby.

"Who's shooting?" Sienna asked, her voice shaking as much as the rest of her.

Ethan didn't answer. He just continued to keep an eye on Franklin because he didn't trust the man one bit.

"Where's Chloe?" Ethan demanded since other than the shooter, she was the only one not accounted for. Of course, she might've been the shooter.

Franklin shook his head. "Last I saw her, she was meeting with someone. A woman with salt-and-pepper hair."

Vernice, no doubt.

"Where were they?" Ethan pressed.

"Chloe's office," Franklin said without hesitation. But Ethan noticed the man was a whole lot steadier than Sienna. In fact, he suddenly looked remarkably calm. "Chloe and I were supposed to have a video appointment with a client in my office at nine thirty. I was headed there when the shooting started."

Ethan wanted to ask if Sienna and he had been together, but that could wait for the interview. He'd need to know Franklin's and Sienna's exact locations when this ordeal had started.

"It's me," someone called out. Rory. "I'm coming your way."

"Here," Ethan replied to let the deputy know their location. "We have Dr. Franklin Voss and a client, Sienna Carrington, on the stairs. Livvy and I have checked all but one room—the doctor's office."

Since the gunshots had come from this side of the house, it was possible the shooter was still inside. And that was why Ethan waited until Rory had joined them before he went to the door.

Livvy moved, too, quickly taking up position on the other side with Rory, and Ethan leaned over and tested the knob. Like the other rooms, it was unlocked. He threw open the door, automatically moving into a shooting stance. Moving in beside him, Rory and Livvy did the same.

Ethan made a sweeping glance around. And he cursed.

There were no scattered files or toppled furniture in here. But there was blood. Lots of it. And it was pooled around the woman lying on the floor.

Damn it.

She was dead. Ethan was sure of that. The gunshot wound to the head had seen to that.

Chloe's now lifeless eyes stared up at him.

# *Chapter Eleven*

Sitting in the break room of the station, Livvy finished yet another statement of her account of a dead woman. The second one in as many days.

And both were connected to New Hope.

Until Livvy had seen Chloe lying dead on the floor, she'd believed Chloe could be a killer. That was possibly still true. She could have murdered Ivy all those years ago and then Zadie when she'd threatened to uncover the truth. But if Chloe was truly guilty, then someone had murdered the killer.

Ethan must have finished his statement, too, because he muttered some profanity under his breath and leaned back from the laptop that he'd been using. Not in Grace's office this time. Things had been too hectic for them to use that space, and they hadn't wanted to do reports in the bullpen, considering Grace had ordered all three of their remaining suspects to come in for questioning.

Franklin, Anthony and Vernice.

Livvy doubted any of them were happy about being interrogated, but with two deaths, Grace had more than just cause. Maybe something would come out in the interviews that would help them solve this case.

Since Ethan was in the chair across from the sofa where

she was sitting, when he looked up, their gazes connected. She managed a smile. Yes, it was barely there, but she wanted to try to assure him that she wasn't on the verge of falling apart. She probably failed big time, but he returned a lukewarm smile of his own.

"I want to know what Vernice was doing at New Hope," he said, voicing something that she, too, wanted. "Whoever questions her will certainly ask about that, but no way is Grace going to allow either of us in that interview."

Livvy nodded in agreement. It was a conflict of interest, which was too bad because she thought she might be able to trigger Vernice's rage just by walking into the room. Riled people often spilled more than the calm, calculated ones.

The baby kicked, snapping her mind away from Vernice. Livvy hadn't meant to grunt, but the movement had been a lot stronger than usual and had surprised her.

"Girl kicks," she said, smiling for real this time. And watching Ethan's reaction.

He didn't give anything away. "Are you sure you don't want to know the sex of the baby? It'll make it easier to narrow down names. Mellie for sure if it's a girl, and if it's a boy, we can come up with a name for him."

She considered letting him tell her the gender. And dismissed it. Then, she took a huge emotional risk: "I think I'd rather you tell me right after a kiss. A kiss like the one at the pasture fence before Vernice showed up."

Again, he didn't react, and Livvy realized she was holding her breath. Heck. Saying that had been a huge mistake. It was too soon. She was pushing too hard. And Ethan wasn't ready for that.

"All right," he finally said.

Livvy blew out her breath and got hit with a whole lot

of relief. Relief that brought on some guilt because she'd pushed Ethan into saying that.

"No kiss required," she backpedaled. She had to give him an out so that it didn't strain their already strained relationship.

"Livvy, kissing you isn't a hardship." But his forehead bunched up, and she saw the slight tightness in his jaw.

No hardship, but it still wasn't easy for him. Not in some ways at least. The attraction drew them together, but most of the time, they were mindless and ruled by lust.

Most of the time.

That caused her to smile again, but the sound of approaching footsteps put a quick end to joy. They set aside their laptops and got to their feet just as Rory came through the door.

He volleyed glances at them, and she didn't think it was her imagination that he was assessing how she was. "I'm fine," Livvy said in a preemptive strike.

"Good." Rory bobbed his head and seemed more than a little relieved about that. "We've got a couple of updates, and I figured you two wouldn't want to wait until the reports were all done."

"You figured right," Ethan let him know.

Rory hitched his thumb toward the hall with the interview rooms. "Franklin and Sienna are here, and Sienna is giving her statement to Eden now. Franklin lawyered up, and we're waiting for him to show."

"He lawyered up to give a statement about his dead sister?" Ethan asked.

Livvy totally understood his surprise. Most people were in too much shock after something like that to ask for their attorney. And most innocent siblings didn't think they needed legal representation for something that wasn't their fault.

So, was Franklin guilty? Or was he just the sort of person who wanted to play it safe?

"The ME gave us some preliminary info on Chloe," Rory went on a moment later. "She died from a single gunshot wound to the head."

"Accidental?" Livvy suggested. "Perhaps hit with a stray bullet the shooter was firing?"

Rory shook his head. "There was stippling on her right temple."

Stippling was the marks caused by gunpowder burning or coming in contact with the skin. That meant Chloe had been shot either point-blank or from a very close range.

Livvy thought of the mess in Chloe's office. It looked as if a struggle could have taken placed there. It was possible that she had run and gone into her brother's office, only to be murdered there.

"Were there defensive wounds on Chloe?" Ethan asked.

This time Rory shrugged. "Possibly. There were red marks on her arms. Maybe from where someone had grabbed her. Bennie and Garrison are getting statements from the staff and clients at New Hope to try to learn if Chloe had recently been injured."

Garrison Zimmer was one of their fellow deputies, and even though he was a rookie, his instincts were good. Added to that, his calm, friendly manner might put the surrogates and others at ease.

"Garrison and Bennie have already done a search of the house and the perimeter, and they found no signs of a shooter," Rory explained. "There are no indications of a break-in either."

"Vernice was there," Ethan pointed out.

"So I heard." Rory checked the time. "She should be coming in soon. Anthony, too. We'll find out if either of them have alibis for the time of the shooting, and we're already getting a warrant to test them for gunshot residue."

Good. Because with Chloe being killed up close, the shooter might have some GSR on their hands or clothes. Of course, if Vernice and Anthony were smart, they would at least have tried to clean themselves up. Franklin, however, wouldn't have gotten the chance.

The three of them turned when there was the sound of yet more footsteps, and Livvy expected to see Grace or one of the other deputies step into the break room. Instead, it was a young woman with pink hair, wearing jeans and a sweatshirt.

"May I help you?" Ethan asked, but it wasn't exactly a welcoming tone. Understandable because this wasn't an area for visitors.

Despite Ethan's gruff tone, the woman smiled. At Livvy. "I'm Nova Bonetti," she said, as if she expected that to ring a bell for Livvy. It didn't. "The sketch artist," she added when she obviously saw the blank look on Livvy's face. Then, the woman took out her ID to show them.

"Oh, I wasn't expecting you until…" Livvy checked the time and groaned softly. "*Now.*" Only then did she recall the appointment that Grace had arranged. "Sorry—we've, uh, had a lot going on this morning."

"Yeah, it looks busy out in the bullpen." Nova hiked her thumb in that direction. "Do you need to reschedule?" she asked.

Livvy debated that. She was exhausted from the spent adrenaline that'd come with the shooting, but this could end up being important. Critical, even, if the images from her nightmares could be matched to a specific person.

Of course, this could be a waste of time if the nightmare hadn't actually happened.

She prayed that it hadn't.

That she hadn't witnessed something so horrific, though Livvy suspected that it wasn't an actual dream but rather memories trying to leak through the gaps in her mind.

"I don't want to reschedule," she let the woman know. But then she considered a good place to do the session. "How about here?" she finally suggested when she realized that all the interview rooms and Grace's office would likely be occupied.

"Works for me," Nova said in a cheerful tone that didn't match the mood of anyone else in the room. Rory and especially Ethan knew this wasn't going to be a piece of cake for her.

"I'll leave you to it," Rory said.

He headed out, easing the door shut behind them. That wouldn't guarantee them any privacy. People came and went from this room all the time, but Rory would no doubt spread the word about what was happening.

"This is Deputy Ethan Oakley," Livvy said, introducing him and shaking Nova's hand. Ethan and she sat on the sofa while Nova took the chair. "And you can call me Livvy."

"All right, Livvy," Nova repeated, opening the backpack she'd brought with her. She didn't take out a sketchpad but rather a tablet. "I don't use digital imaging software," she explained. "I do the drawing from what you can tell me. So, relax, take a few deep breaths and try to clear your mind so you can focus better."

Livvy dragged in a few breaths and did her best to tune out the past hours and home in on the past.

"Just start with the basics," Nova instructed, "and we'll adjust as we go."

"A woman," Livvy managed. "In her late twenties or early thirties. Slim build. Blond hair cut short and choppy. Green eyes. An oval-shaped face with no distinguishing marks," she added as Nova got to work. "A slight cleft in her chin. Beautiful," she murmured. "She was beautiful."

Nova made a brief glance up from her screen. "*Was*," she repeated. She didn't seem unnerved by that fact, only curious. "How long had she been dead when you saw her?"

Livvy had to shake her head.

"All right, then I won't be able to estimate skin tone," she said as she just kept working. "Tell me about her cheekbones and jaw."

Livvy didn't have to conjure up the images. They were already front and center in her mind. "Neither was pronounced. Average."

"And her mouth?" Nova went on.

"Full," she provided.

Nova looked up again. "Like yours?"

She settled for a nod, and she was glad when Ethan reached over and took her hand.

"And the shape of the eyes?" Nova pressed.

"Round with just a slight upturn at the edges."

Nova worked in silence for a few minutes, her pen quickly moving over the tablet's screen. She then turned it for Livvy to see. Livvy released the breath she'd been holding when she saw that it wasn't the woman's face. Not quite.

"Her cheeks are slightly fuller," she supplied. "And her hair was a darker blond."

Nova immediately got started on tweaking the image, and when she was done, she turned it back toward Livvy. There was another round of minor adjustments on the position of the eyes. One on the curve of her chin, too. But when Nova added in all of those and showed her the sketch, Livvy knew they'd nailed it.

"Yes," she managed. "That's the woman."

Nova beamed out a smile, which faded considerably when she saw Livvy's reaction. "All right," she murmured. "I'll fire off a copy of this to the sheriff. I'm guessing you'll want one as well."

"I do," Livvy said, and she gave Nova her phone number. Nova immediately sent a text with the picture attached.

Ethan took her phone and looked at the image. He muttered something under his breath that she didn't catch.

"I can go ahead and put this in the missing persons database," he offered, and when Livvy nodded, he sent off the image. Now all that was left was the waiting. If they got a hit, they'd know who she was, and if they didn't, then they were back to square one.

"Thank you," Livvy told Nova as the woman gathered up her things and got to her feet.

"Anytime." She tipped her head toward Livvy's phone, where the sketch was still on the screen. "Hope you find her," Nova added.

Both Ethan and Livvy stood, following Nova out of the break room and back toward the bullpen. They said their goodbyes, and she headed to the front door.

Just as Anthony walked in.

Livvy didn't have to guess the man's mood. The muscles in Anthony's face and his mouth were tight. His eyes were narrowed, and he aimed those eyes at Ethan and her.

"Why the hell was I ordered to come in again?" Anthony snapped.

Livvy sighed. "Because we need to ask you some questions."

He spewed out some raw profanity while he made his

way through the metal detector. "You want to harass me, that's what. You think I killed Chloe. I didn't. But I'm not sorry she's gone. Chloe got exactly what was coming to her."

"Which means you had motive to murder her," Ethan pointed out. "And before you say anything else, let me refresh your Miranda warning."

Ethan proceeded to do just that while Anthony glared at them and spouted off more of that profanity. The chatter must have alerted Grace because she opened her office door. She had her phone to her ear but issued an "I'll get back to you" to the caller. She ended the call and looked at Anthony.

"You're the one who ordered me in," Anthony complained, but he didn't give Grace a chance to confirm that. "And here I should be celebrating that witch's death instead of being hauled in here to be grilled."

"This way," she insisted, waggling her fingers for Anthony to follow her. "Livvy and Ethan, you're welcome to join us."

They took Grace up on that offer and entered her office. Probably because the interview rooms were all still occupied. Grace immediately went to her printer to retrieve something that she then put on her desk. Livvy saw that it was a copy of the sketch she'd just done with Nova.

"I printed it out so I could have a better look at it," Grace muttered to her as they were taking their seats. "Thanks for doing that. I know it couldn't have been easy for you."

Livvy nodded. It hadn't been easy, but in hindsight, it was something she should have done years ago. It was time she faced the truth.

Whatever that truth might be.

Grace sat behind her desk, and she hit the recording

function on her phone before shifting her attention to Anthony. She was doling out just as much of a glare as he was while she read in the pertinent time, place and those present for the interview.

"Mr. Carlton, tell us your whereabouts this morning," Grace started.

"Well, I sure as hell wasn't at New Hope shooting Chloe." Smugness replaced his glare. That didn't last, though, because of Grace's withering stare. "All right, fine. I was at home."

"Can anyone corroborate that?" Grace was quick to ask.

"No." He didn't seem bothered about that either. "I guess you'll just have to take my word for it."

She shrugged. "Or I can do a gunshot-residue test to see if you recently fired a gun."

Something went across Anthony's face. Alarm, maybe. "Don't you need a warrant for that?"

Grace lifted a paper from her desk. "Which I have. Just a few more questions, and then I'll do the swab—"

"I fired a gun," Anthony blurted. "Not at New Hope," he was quick to add. "But at Hannigan's."

Livvy knew the place. It was one of those massive sporting goods stores outside of San Antonio that had a firing range.

"So, you just happened to shoot a gun there at the same time there was an attack at New Hope?" Grace asked, the skepticism coating her voice.

"No, it didn't just happen," Anthony snarled. "After what happened to Zadie, I wanted to buy a gun for protection."

"When I view the surveillance feed for Hannigan's, you'll be on it?" Grace pressed.

"Yes," Anthony said without hesitation. "I was there yesterday."

She lifted an eyebrow. "And you bought a gun?"

"I did," he verified. "It's in the glove compartment of my car."

After a glance from Grace, Ethan took out his phone. "Should I go ahead and get started on a warrant to confiscate the gun and examine it?"

"Absolutely." She paused a heartbeat. "Unless Anthony will voluntarily let us look at it and check to see if it matches the caliber of the shots fired at New Hope."

Anthony opened his mouth but then seemed to change his mind about what he'd been about to say. "Tit for tat," he threw out there. "I'll give you permission to test my gun if you'll give me back my mother's diary."

The comment clearly surprised Grace. "The diary is still being analyzed," she let him know.

"Well, I want it back now," Anthony demanded. "I should have never let it out of my hands."

Livvy heard a lot of regret in the man's voice. And worry. Grace no doubt picked up on that, too.

"There are some inconsistencies in the diary," she informed him, "and it's being checked to see if it's valid. There are tests to determine the age of the ink."

Again, Anthony opened his mouth, stopped and then cursed. He groaned but managed to keep a defiant expression.

"All right, full disclosure," he finally said, holding up his hands. "I wrote parts of the diary."

"Really?" Grace stretched out the syllables on that. "Why would you do something like that?"

He huffed. "Because I wanted to draw out my mother's killer. I wanted to draw out Chloe. I didn't want her dead," he was quick to add. "I wanted her to admit what she'd done, and I thought the diary would get you to arrest her."

"Or I could arrest you for falsifying evidence and obstruction of justice," Grace fired back.

That put some panic in Anthony's eyes, and he stayed quiet for several moments before he snapped out, "I want a lawyer."

Grace pulled in a long breath but then nodded. She motioned for him to stand. "You can make that call and then wait in reception. You won't be leaving the building until you've finished this interview."

"Are you arresting me?" he grumbled.

"Not at this moment. Don't give me a reason to change my mind about that," Grace warned him.

Anthony cursed her and stormed out, nearly knocking into Eden, who was right by the door. Eden gave him a long cop's glance before she motioned for Grace, Livvy and Ethan to go back into Grace's office.

"I just finished taking Sienna's statement," Eden explained. "She says she was in her quarters on the top floor when she heard the shots, and at first she thought it was a car backfiring or a TV on too loud. Sienna said when the noise continued, she made her way down the back stairs, where you found her." Eden glanced at Livvy and Ethan.

"Where we found her. And Franklin," Livvy emphasized.

Eden nodded. "Yeah, about that. Sienna says Franklin didn't join her there on the stairs until after the shots had stopped. And get this—Franklin asked Sienna to do him a favor and to tell everyone that he'd been with her during the entire time of the shooting."

"So, he asked her to lie," Grace muttered, and she smiled. "Sounds like grounds for an arrest to me. Since

Franklin's lawyer got here about ten minutes ago, we can start the interview. Come on," she added to Livvy and Ethan. "Let's see what Franklin has to say."

# *Chapter Twelve*

Ethan wished he could ask Livvy to sit out this interview. She was no doubt still rattled after giving the details for that sketch. Heck, rattled as well because of the gunfire they'd gotten caught up in at New Hope only a few hours ago.

But there was no way Livvy would miss the chance to question one of their key suspects, and Franklin had zoomed to the top of that suspect list by asking Sienna to lie for him.

Ethan thought of the mess he'd seen in Chloe's office. Had the brother and sister gotten into an argument there, one that had turned violent after Chloe had followed Franklin into his office? Maybe. But it was also possible that Franklin had had no part in it and that he had another reason for wanting Sienna to lie for him. Ethan hoped they would have answers about that soon.

Grace, Livvy and he stepped into the interview room, and Ethan immediately spotted Franklin having a whispered conversation with a brunette woman in a navy business suit. She was probably only in her early thirties, but she had a no-nonsense, seasoned expression that Ethan had often seen in veteran attorneys.

"My client is grieving the death of his sister," the lawyer was quick to say. "He's in shock. I want you to make this fast so he can go home and start making arrangements for her funeral."

"Things would have gone a lot quicker if we hadn't had to wait for you to show up," Grace fired back. "And as for a funeral, that won't be happening any time soon, so you have plenty of time to plan it. This is a murder investigation, and it can take weeks for the body to be released."

That clearly didn't please the lawyer, but Franklin didn't react. Ethan noted that he didn't appear to be in shock either.

Grace ignored the woman's steely look and turned on the recorder. "Sheriff Grace Granger, Deputy Livvy Walsh and Deputy Ethan Oakley in an interview with Dr. Franklin Voss and his attorney. Could you please state your name?" she added, glancing at the brunette.

"Helene Barrett," she provided, and she rattled off the name of her impressive-sounding law firm.

Grace added the date and time for the sake of the recording, and then the three of them sat across the table from Franklin and his lawyer. Ethan instantly caught a whiff of something coming off Franklin and recognized it as the soap in the bathroom just up the hall. It was so strong that it was almost as if Franklin had bathed in the darn stuff.

Or tried to wash away gunshot residue.

Even though Grace was obviously ready to start, Ethan jotted down a note about the soap and jacket, and he passed it to Grace. She nodded when she read it and then pinned her attention to Franklin.

"Dr. Voss, did you happen to scrub your hands in the bathroom?" she asked.

Franklin looked puzzled. Or rather pretended he was

anyway. "I'm a doctor. I make a habit of thoroughly washing my hands."

The lawyer huffed. "Why are you asking that? What does it have to do with why we're here?"

"It could have everything to do with why we're here," Grace admitted, not looking at Helene but rather Franklin. "What about your jacket? Where is it?"

Franklin sat up straighter in the chair. "At New Hope. I took it off before your deputy put me in a cruiser and brought me here."

The lawyer's next huff was even louder, and she added an eye roll to it. But Grace ignored it. "Tell us where you put the jacket because it'll need to be examined," she remarked. "It's standard procedure."

"It is only if you think my client is a killer," the lawyer piped in with that irritating tone that made Ethan want to curse. "He's not. He's a distinguished physician with a stellar reputation."

"One who was on scene at his sister's murder," Ethan reminded her. "Clothing can pick up fibers and trace evidence. The jacket could help ID Chloe's killer. And we all want that, don't we?"

There. Ethan had thrown the ball into their court. If Franklin refused to cooperate now, it would show he wasn't willing to do everything possible to get justice for Chloe.

Franklin didn't say anything for several seconds, but finally muttered "Yes, we do all want that" through clenched teeth. "That jacket is somewhere in the parlor, I think. I tossed it there on my way out, and that means it's probably contaminated as far as collecting potential evidence from it."

That was true, and Ethan had to wonder if the *contamination* had been intentional on Franklin's part. Or he could just be reading the doctor wrong. Maybe Franklin hadn't actually had any part in killing his sister but rather just wasn't that torn up about her being dead.

"Still, even if someone else has touched the jacket, the CSIs will locate it and examine it," Grace assured Franklin, and she fired off a text, no doubt to get that process started. "Now, tell us where you were when the shots were fired," she continued once she'd finished with the message.

Franklin looked annoyed with the request. "Like I already told your two deputies, Chloe and I were supposed to have a video appointment with a client in my office at nine thirty. I was headed there and ran into Sienna when the shots started." He looked at Ethan and Livvy. "You saw us."

"Were you with Sienna the whole time shots were going off?" Livvy jumped in to ask.

For a moment Franklin got a deer-in-the-headlights look, and he studied the three of them, maybe trying to see if they knew about him telling Sienna to lie for him. With his jaw tightening even more, Franklin leaned in closer to his lawyer, cupping his hands around his mouth, and they had a brief whispered conversation. When they were done, it was the lawyer who answered.

"My client was with Sienna for part of the time," Helene stated.

"*Part*," Grace repeated, sounding all cop. "Had the shots actually stopped by the time you joined Sienna on the stairs?"

That prompted another muffled conversation between Franklin and his lawyer. While they chatted, Grace took out her phone again. "I'm sure I have Sienna's statement here to check to see what she has to say about that. You know, to make sure it meshes with what you're about to say."

If looks could have killed, both Helene and Franklin would have ended all three of them then and there. "My client doesn't know if the shots had stopped when he joined Sienna on the stairs. He was in shock, terrified for his life and his client's. By then, he'd put his hands over his ears to block out the horrific sounds."

Ethan raised an eyebrow and stared at Franklin and her. He made sure they saw that he knew that was a lie.

"You know, telling the truth, the whole truth and nothing but the truth is a big deal in interview," Ethan reminded him. "Facts and honesty will help us find the killer. And the sooner we do that, the sooner the media will back off covering the story. It can't be good for business to have headlines like *Murder at New Hope* splashed all around."

"My client is telling the truth," Helene snapped.

Ethan shrugged and shifted his gaze to Franklin. "Give us your movements for the morning, prior to the shooting," he insisted.

Franklin didn't seem relieved by the slight shift in questioning. "I got up at six as I always do, worked out on the treadmill and had breakfast. Then, at about seven thirty, I got ready for work and went downstairs to my office."

"Did you see Chloe?" Livvy asked.

"Yes. She was going into her office with the woman I told you about. The one with salt-and-pepper hair."

"Where exactly were you when you heard the first shot?" Ethan wanted to know.

That brought another of those blasted whispered conversations with his lawyer before Franklin answered. "On the third floor. I'd gone up to check and see if the new client quarters were ready. We've had some issues with our housekeeping services. When I heard the shot, I was already on my way downstairs for my meeting, and that's when I saw Sienna."

Considering there were two other sets of stairs in the house, Franklin could have fired those shots and then created an alibi of sorts for himself by joining Sienna. Of course, there was no evidence to back that up.

Not yet anyway.

"Do you know who ransacked your sister's office?" Grace continued.

He gave a quick shake of his head, followed by a lift of his shoulder. "Maybe that woman who visited her this morning. Is she the one who killed Chloe?" he asked, as if the idea had just occurred to him.

Grace used her phone to pull up Vernice's picture. "Was it this woman?" she asked.

"Yes, that's her all right. Did she kill my sister?" he pressed.

"We're looking into that along with some other persons of interest," Grace assured him. "Had you seen her before?"

Franklin's forehead bunched up while he gave that some thought. "Yes. I recall her coming to New Hope on at least one other occasion. I assumed she was a friend of Chloe's."

"Or she could have killed her," the lawyer piped in. "I hope you're grilling her the way you are my client."

Grace made a sound that could have meant anything. "Dr. Voss, could you please tell me about the house where Zadie's body was found?" she said, obviously switching things up again.

"The house?" he questioned, clearly surprised. "I don't know what you mean. I don't know anything about it."

"That's odd." Grace pulled up something on her phone. "Because New Hope once owned it."

The lawyer and Franklin exchanged a glance. "I wasn't aware of that," he said just as Helene snarled, "What does this have to do with the shooting today?"

Grace gave her a flat look. "You really have to ask?" And she didn't wait for the lawyer to respond. "Two women, both connected to New Hope, have been murdered. A third, Sunny Covington, was attacked, and someone attempted to murder her. Everything regarding New Hope needs to be scrutinized. Including the property where Zadie's body was found."

"Zadie," Franklin murmured, and he squeezed his eyes shut a moment. For the first time since the interview started, the man showed what Ethan thought might be actual grief. "Such a loss. But you have her killer, right? It's the same man who tried to attack Sunny at the hospital?"

Grace made another of those sounds that gave away nothing of what she was actually thinking. "Did you know Hank Stover, the man who tried to kill Sunny?"

"No," Franklin replied without hesitation.

"Strange," she commented. "His sister used to work for you, and he visited New Hope."

He sighed. "We've had a lot of employees and visitors over the years, and I don't recall ever seeing that man." He paused a moment. "How is Sunny?" he asked. "When will I be able to visit her?"

"We're restricting visitors for the time being," Grace said, obviously not addressing the doctor's first question.

Franklin's mouth went into a tight line, his lips pinching together for several moments. "Sunny will want to see me," he insisted.

Grace ignored that, too, and checked something else on

her phone. "Dr. Voss, there's a rumor that you've fathered some of the babies born via surrogates at New Hope."

"What?" Franklin howled.

His lawyer gave his arm a quick squeeze. Clearly a signal for him to hush. Franklin did, but Helene sure didn't.

"That is just a rumor, nothing more, and has nothing to do with his sister's death," she insisted.

"It could," Livvy supplied. "Someone ransacked Chloe's office, maybe looking for something incriminating. That could have included allegations about the paternity of some of the babies conceived at New Hope."

"And you're on a fishing expedition," Helene spat out, and her voice was ice cold. Ditto for the glare she shot Livvy.

Livvy made an odd sound, and Ethan glanced at her. Something was wrong. She had gone pale. Hell. What had happened? Was something wrong with the baby? Maybe she was in pain. Ethan reached out his hand to her, but Livvy shook her head.

Obviously, Grace didn't notice, though, because she pulled up something else on her phone. "Take a look at this," she said, showing it to Franklin. It was the sketch Nova had created. "Does she look familiar?"

Something went through Franklin's eyes. Not the fury he'd been tossing at them. But some emotion that Ethan couldn't quite put his finger on. He wanted to know what, but more than that, he needed to know if Livvy was okay.

"Uh, I need a moment with my lawyer," Franklin said. "Could you give us some privacy?"

"Interview paused," Grace replied for the sake of the recording.

She switched off the recorder, and Ethan walked out

behind Livvy and Grace. The moment the door was shut, he stepped in front of Livvy.

"What happened in there? What's wrong?" Ethan demanded. "Is it the baby?"

Grace looked at Livvy, too, and she muttered some profanity under her breath. "Are you all right?" she blurted, obviously seeing how little color there was in Livvy's face.

"It's not the baby," Livvy assured them, and she swallowed hard. "When Franklin was talking, something flashed in my mind. Nothing having to do with the investigation or the nightmare," she added. "I think it was an actual memory."

That got Ethan's attention. Grace's, too. "Of what?" Grace asked.

"From when I was a child." Livvy's voice was trembling now, and Ethan slid his arm around her. "I was at New Hope. I was on those stairs where we saw Franklin and Sienna."

Ethan had heard her go over every single detail of the nightmare and her childhood, but he'd never once heard her mention anything about being at New Hope. Or recognizing those stairs.

"I wasn't alone," Livvy continued after pulling in a long breath. "There was someone with me." She lifted her head, her gaze locking with Ethan's. "The woman from the sketch. The dead woman who I saw in the bathtub." Her voice broke. "God, Ethan. I think I stabbed her."

# *Chapter Thirteen*

Livvy felt the dread and guilt slam through her. So much of it that it might have brought her to her knees.

Ethan made sure that didn't happen though.

He kept hold of her, and he got her moving away from the interview room. Grace followed along, and none of them said anything else until they were in her office and the door was shut.

"Sit down," Grace ordered, and she went to the mini fridge in the corner of her office to get a bottle of water. She opened it and had Livvy drink some before she sat behind her desk.

Ethan took the chair next to Livvy, and he continued to keep his arm around her. Steadying her. Once again, he was there for her.

"What makes you think you killed this woman?" Grace asked.

Livvy took in another long breath. Maybe it was Ethan or the exhaustion, but she felt an odd sort of peace come over her.

She had remembered something.

Something real, something from her actual past. Despite what she had recalled, it felt like, well, progress. The trouble was this was no doubt the tip of the proverbial iceberg, and the next thing she remembered might not be sitting in a stairwell at New Hope.

It might be plunging a knife into someone.

"I obviously knew her," Livvy said as she tried to answer Grace's question. "She was on the stairs with me. We were sort of cowering there, I suppose." She stopped and glanced at the way Ethan's arm was looped around her. "Sort of like this."

"With the woman comforting you?" Grace suggested.

Livvy considered that, and then she had to shake her head. "I can't be certain, but in that flash of an image, I'm holding a knife. And I think it was the one that Vernice brought in."

Ethan and Grace stayed quiet a moment. "Were you afraid of the woman? Did you think she was going to harm you?" he asked.

Livvy knew where he was going with this. If she had stabbed her, he wanted it to be self-defense. And maybe it had been.

"I'm not sure if I was scared of her or just the situation we were in," she had to admit again. "I think we were hiding from something or someone, but why would I have had the knife? As an adult, why didn't she have it?"

"Plenty of reasons," Ethan was quick to say, and he proceeded to name some possibilities. "You'd found it. Or grabbed it because you were terrified. The woman could have given it to you to hold because she had a different kind of weapon, maybe even a gun. There's also the possibility that it might not have even been a real knife or the one that Vernice brought us."

"All of that could be true," Livvy admitted. But even if she hadn't used the knife to attack someone or defend herself, there were still other questions. She voiced two of them. "Who was the woman, and why were the two of us at New Hope?"

"Franklin might be able to answer that," Grace remarked.

Livvy nodded. "Yes, he possibly could, but only if it doesn't incriminate him in some way."

"There's that," Grace grumbled. "And his legal watchdog is keeping a tight leash on him. He'll probably go in the *deny, deny, deny* mode." She sighed and got to her feet. "Still, he wanted to have a chat with his lawyer about that sketch that I showed him, so he might be ready to spill something."

That was a huge *might.* Because even if it didn't directly incriminate him, Livvy figured that Franklin would do pretty much anything to keep New Hope from coming under any more scrutiny.

"All right, I'll finish up the interview with Franklin," Grace said, starting for the door. "Just an FYI—unless he confesses, I'll have to let him go. I don't have enough evidence to make an arrest."

Livvy knew that. Heck, they didn't have enough to hold Anthony on murder charges even though Grace could charge him with obstruction and a few other crimes. Since Anthony didn't have a record, he'd likely be out on bail within an hour or two.

Grace walked out, closing the door behind herself. Livvy looked at Ethan, ready to assure him that she was all right so he wouldn't worry. But he stopped anything she was about to say by brushing his mouth over hers.

It was barely a kiss. Or rather it would have been had it come from anyone else, but coming from Ethan, it was still amazing. Still hot enough to push aside some of that dread that had taken over her body.

"You're a good person," he said, his voice a low, soothing murmur. "And you were a good person when you were a kid. I want you to remember that because I know bone deep that whatever happened with that knife, you did what you had to do. Not out of maliciousness or evil but out of survival. Or because you were protecting someone," he added.

That last part hadn't occurred to Livvy. But yes, it could be that. Had she been trying to protect the woman with her on the stairs? Maybe. If so, how had she ended up dead in that bathtub?

"I need to know why I was at New Hope," Livvy said on a sigh.

Ethan nodded and took the laptop from Grace's desk. He froze for a second when his attention landed on something. On the sketch, she realized.

Livvy looked at the drawing again now, trying to study it with an objective eye. Hard to do since there was so much emotion involved in this, but she compared it to the memory flash she'd had.

"Yes, I'm certain this is the woman who was on the stairs with me," she managed to say.

"And maybe that woman will be on the list Eden put together," Ethan reminded her. He sat back down beside her, opening the master list.

Obviously, some research had already been done since there were now notes by some of the names. The first one, Heather Donnelly, for instance had died from cancer a year earlier. Another one, who'd been a nurse at New Hope, was in her eighties and had dementia.

"Look through the list," Ethan instructed, "and see if anything rings a bell."

She did. Livvy looked at every name, hoping there

would be some sliver of recognition. But there wasn't, and her frustrated sigh must have conveyed that to Ethan.

"It's all right," he assured her. "It was a long shot. There are no doubt plenty of other surrogates, clients and employees who aren't even on this list." He paused a moment. "There's also the possibility that the woman used an alias."

That was true, and it brought on another wave of frustration. Frustration that Ethan obviously picked up on.

"This list is just a start," he insisted. "More names will be added as the interviews are conducted."

Again, he was right. "Thank you," she said, making the mistake of looking at him again.

Whenever emotions were running this high, defenses were down, which meant she didn't hide her feelings for him. She thought it would cause him to take a mental step back.

It didn't.

Ethan leaned in and kissed her again. And he made this one count even more than the last one. His mouth moved over hers as he knew exactly how to fire up every inch of her body.

Part of Livvy, the part that was guarding her heart, warned her not to dive right in. To hold back and protect herself.

That didn't happen.

Livvy slid her hand around the back of his neck, pulling him even closer to her and deepening the kiss.

Ethan made a rough sound that came from deep within his throat, and without breaking the mouth-to-mouth contact, he put the laptop back on Grace's desk. In the same motion, he snapped Livvy to him until her breasts were pressed against his chest.

It was an amazing feeling, as if all her senses had been

heightened, and she suddenly wanted him even more than that night when they'd landed in bed.

Not good.

For one thing, they were in Grace's office, not at his house. And for another, this heat was a delicious distraction. One that she wanted to slip right into and never come out. But she couldn't do that. Not with so many things undecided between Ethan and her.

Not when they were looking for a killer.

With tons of regret, Livvy eased back from him, and she had no trouble seeing both the heat and the regret in his eyes, too. He sighed and scrubbed his hand over his face.

"When this is done," he said, "when we have the answers we need, then we can work this out between us."

Livvy liked the sound of that. Things had been uncertain between them for too long now. But that uncertainty would have to wait because she wanted to do some work on the list. The sooner they found out what was going on, then Sunny and others, including them, would be a whole lot safer.

She used her phone to access info on one of the names from their portion of the list, but Livvy had barely gotten started when there was a knock at the door. The visitor didn't wait for a response though. The door opened, and Livvy turned to see the woman standing there.

Vernice.

Great. Livvy hadn't steeled herself up nearly enough for this, but she quickly did so. And judging from the scowl Vernice shot them, steeling up would be required.

The woman slid glances at them, especially at the way they were seated. Their arms were still touching, and there wasn't much distance between them. It was also possible that Ethan and she still had the flush of arousal on their faces from that scorching kiss.

"You put Grace up to dragging me in here for questioning," Vernice insisted.

Sighing, Ethan got to his feet. "I didn't have to. All persons of interest are being questioned."

Vernice's mouth opened, and the woman seemed genuinely shocked, no doubt because "person of interest" was the same as "suspect" in her mind.

"What have you told Grace about me?" she demanded as she stepped into the office and shut the door. She volleyed glares at both of them.

Livvy went with the truth. "Grace knows that you were at New Hope earlier today, right before Chloe was gunned down. And she also knows that wasn't your first visit there."

Ethan picked up the explanation. "It's possible you're the last person to see Chloe alive." But he held up his hand to stop Vernice when she started to speak. "Let me go ahead and Mirandize you, and that way whatever you say will become part of your official statement."

Vernice dropped back a step and she reached for the doorknob, but she didn't leave. "Isabel is turning over in her grave because of what you're doing."

Ethan ignored her, though Livvy figured that had to sting, and he turned on the record function on his phone before he recited the Miranda warning. "Do you understand your rights?" he asked when he was finished.

"I understand that you never deserved my daughter," Vernice spat out. "You are despicable. Both of you."

Ethan kept his hard stare on the woman. "Do you understand your legal rights? And FYI, I'll keep asking that until I get a straight answer."

Vernice's eyes went to slits. "I understand my rights." Her voice was low and menacing, a nasty tangle of grief and hatred. Hatred now aimed at Ethan and Livvy.

She didn't care much to be on someone's hate list, but in this case, she figured there was no way around it. As far as Vernice was concerned, Ethan should stay faithful to his late wife forever.

"The sheriff will ask you this in your interview," Ethan went on a moment later, "but tell us why you were at New Hope this morning."

With the way Vernice's lips stayed pinched together, Livvy figured the woman would just clam up. But she didn't. "I've known Chloe for a while now. She's helped several friends of mine with their infertility issues."

Livvy considered that. "So, why visit Chloe this morning?" she pressed when Vernice didn't continue.

"Because obviously someone is trying to drag me into…well, whatever the heck is going on," she ranted. "I mean, why leave the knife on my doorstep? Why pull me into something that clearly isn't my business?" Vernice stopped, and the short tirade seemed to have sapped some of her fury. "I wanted to talk with Chloe and find out if she knew what was going on."

"And did she?" Ethan was quick to ask.

Vernice sighed and shook her head. "She said she didn't. But I don't know Chloe well enough to tell if she was lying."

"Where did you talk with her?" Livvy pressed.

"In one of the front rooms," she replied without hesitation. "I think she called it the parlor."

Ethan continued to stare at her. "Not her office?"

Vernice shook her head and groaned softly. "We talked for about five minutes, and I didn't go anywhere else in the house. I left. And then when I got back to town, I heard about the shooting."

Livvy thought of what Vernice had just said about not knowing Chloe well enough to detect if she was lying. Well, she felt the same way about Vernice. The woman might not be telling the truth about anything. Hopefully, Grace would be able to determine that once she had her in an interview room.

"I didn't kill Chloe," Vernice said as she started pacing in the short space between the side of Grace's desk and the door. "I have no reason to do…" She stopped when her attention landed on something.

Livvy shifted and saw that Vernice was staring at the sketch that Grace had printed out. And not just staring at it either. It was as if Vernice couldn't take her eyes off of it.

"Do you recognize her?" Livvy had to ask.

Vernice didn't respond for a long time before finally tearing her attention from it. "No," she insisted.

But Livvy wasn't convinced. Apparently, neither was Ethan. "You're sure? Because you look as if you've seen a ghost."

She did, and that stark shock continued in Vernice's eyes as she looked at Livvy. "I don't know her," the woman muttered, and this time she did head to the door. She threw it open with far more force than necessary.

"I'll wait for Grace out here," she muttered, slamming the door shut behind herself.

Livvy considered going after the woman, to press her for what she knew. And Vernice obviously knew something, or she wouldn't have reacted that way.

"I need to let Grace know about this," Ethan said, jotting down some notes that he would no doubt pass along to her before she took Vernice into the interview.

He had just finished writing when there was another knock at the door. At first Livvy thought that Vernice had returned, but when she opened it, Rory was standing there. One look at his face, and she knew something was wrong.

"What happened?" she asked.

But Rory didn't respond until he was in the office and had closed the door. "I just got off the phone with the lab. They got the results back on the knife that was left at Vernice's. Results on the traces of blood," he clarified.

Livvy's heart started to tighten into a knot. "I'm guessing they got a match?" she managed to say.

Rory nodded but then shrugged. "Not exactly, but there's a familial match in the system."

Her head was suddenly whirling, making it hard to think, and her blank expression was probably why he spelled it all out.

"A familial match points to a close biological relative of the unknown DNA," Rory said, the sympathy practically seeping off him. "A match to you, Livvy. The lab techs believe the blood on that knife belongs to your mother."

# *Chapter Fourteen*

Ethan watched as Livvy sat in his kitchen, eating the salad they'd picked up from the town's diner on the way back to his house. It was obvious from her expression that she wasn't enjoying the late lunch, that she was merely going through the motions.

He figured she was eating solely for the baby, and he suspected if she hadn't been pregnant, she would have just gone somewhere alone to try to process what Rory had told them. Ethan was trying to process it, too, and while they now had an answer as to whose blood was on that knife, it had only fueled more questions.

Who was Livvy's mother? Was she dead?

And if so, who had killed her?

Yeah, plenty of questions, including how the hell had the knife ended up being delivered to Vernice? Or maybe it hadn't been delivered after all. It was possible that Vernice had had it all this time but had chosen to give it to the cops because she could have known it would incriminate Livvy since her prints were also on it.

He ate some of the burger that had also come from the diner and realized he was going through the motions of eating, too. He wasn't the least bit hungry. Not with his stomach in knots over what Livvy was going through.

But his body needed the fuel so he could continue the investigation.

Unfortunately, his heart wasn't in doing that either, but he had his laptop open on the counter and was reviewing the list Eden had given them. He definitely wasn't making much progress and hadn't found squat that would help them with those answers they desperately needed.

Livvy grunted a little, and she put her hand on her belly. "More kicks," she muttered, no doubt when she saw the alarm skirt across his face.

Good timing, Ethan thought, because that seemed to snap her back to the moment. A moment where there hopefully wasn't any images of her nightmare.

But there obviously was.

"It's likely my mother was the dead woman in the bathtub," Livvy said, causing him to sigh. He reached for her, but she shook her head. "If you hold me now, I'll break. And that can't happen. Because I don't need to think like a traumatized six-year-old girl. I need to think like a cop."

He considered that, nodded. Of the two, cop mode was preferable. Because he didn't want her to break.

"Of our three suspects, Anthony would have been too young to have the motive to kill my mother," Livvy spelled out. "He would have only been ten at the time."

"He could have had motive," Ethan argued. "If he thought your mother had some part in killing his, then Anthony could have perhaps managed it."

She conceded that with a nod. "But why not just go after Chloe instead? It was obvious during interview that he believed she had murdered his mother because the woman was jealous of the attention her husband was paying her."

"Anthony might have thought both were involved. Or

he could have said that to throw us off his scent if he had killed when he was ten."

Ethan tried to play that out, and he just couldn't wrap his head around a kid doing that. Not just the murder but then taking the knife that had Livvy's prints on it. Most kids, unless they were budding cold-blooded killers, would have dropped the knife.

And maybe Anthony had done just that.

Dropped it, and somehow it'd gotten into Vernice's hands.

"Franklin could have motive," Livvy went on several moments later. "My mother could have found something incriminating about him or New Hope. That could have been why she and I were cowering in the stairwell near Franklin's office. She could have run with me, and Franklin could have found us and killed her." She paused. "But then why not just kill me, too?"

"Hell," Ethan spat out.

He hated thinking about this. The nightmare that had actually happened. And heaven knew what Livvy had witnessed that'd caused her mind to shut down.

She reached out, took hold of his hand and gave it a gentle squeeze. Comforting him. He cursed again because he should've been the one comforting her.

"It helps to focus on it like a cop," she explained.

Maybe. But this didn't feel like helping. It felt as if they were jabbing at old wounds. Still, it had to be done because this was how the case could end up being solved.

"Anthony could have killed my mother," Livvy went on. "Franklin could have, too. That leaves us with Vernice."

Yeah, it did. "Vernice, who's lied about her connection to New Hope. And she had possession of the knife."

He stopped, considering something. "Has Vernice always been…hostile to you, even when you were a kid?"

Livvy didn't hesitate. She nodded. "Nothing obvious, but I always had the feeling she didn't like me. As I got older, I thought maybe that was because you and I were close friends and she didn't want that to develop into something more since you were with her daughter."

"That could have played into it," he admitted. "But what if Vernice was worried your memory would return and you could implicate her in some way?"

She didn't get a chance to answer because his phone rang, and when he saw Grace's name on the screen, he answered it right away on speaker.

"How's Livvy?" Grace asked the moment she was on the line. "And give me the truth and not what you want me to hear."

"I'm, uh, trying to deal with what I remembered and my mother's blood being on the knife," she admitted. "I'm probably not dealing well, but I'll get there."

He hoped that was true. Ethan wanted Livvy to be able to get past this and not be in so much emotional torment.

"Did you remember anything else?" Grace pressed.

"No, but Ethan and I were just going over how that piece of memory might fit with our suspects."

"Good. Keep doing that because we need a break in this case." Grace sighed, the frustration coming through loud and clear. "I haven't done the reports yet for the interviews with Franklin, Anthony and Vernice, but I wanted you to know that nothing else came out that we can use. As expected, I had to cut them all loose."

Ethan felt his own new wave of frustration though he had known this would be the likely outcome. An outcome where a possible killer was loose and maybe ready to strike again.

"How did Franklin address the accusations about him having fathered some of the babies at New Hope?" Livvy asked.

"He dismissed it as a vicious rumor, and his lawyer threatened a slander suit for ruining Franklin's good name. Blah, blah, blah," Grace muttered. "And since we don't have any actual proof that it did happen, I had to drop it."

"There could possibly be proof," Livvy said, and there was something in her, some tension, that had him looking at her.

Damn it.

He realized then what Livvy was worried about. Maybe Franklin had fathered *her*.

"Is Franklin's DNA in the system?" Ethan came out and asked Grace.

"No," she answered so quickly that it let Ethan know she'd already considered this possibility. "Not yet anyway. I asked for a DNA sample for elimination purposes. His lawyer said we'd need a court order, so I'm in the process of getting one. And I will get it," she insisted.

She no doubt would. It was standard procedure in this type of investigation to be able to rule out any DNA and fingerprints present at a crime scene that could have inadvertently been left there by family members or others in the household.

"It could be telling that Franklin didn't want to cough up his DNA," Grace went on. "But it's also possible that he was just being an uncooperative jerk who doesn't care diddly about his sister's murder being solved."

Yes, either of those could be true.

"Moving on," she continued a moment later. "I just

learned that Anthony possibly knew our dead attacker, Hank Stover. It's a thin connection, but it's there. They lived in the same neighborhood when Anthony was in high school. Of course, Anthony claims he never met the man, so now we're digging to find out if that's a lie."

Since Anthony hadn't been truthful with them so far, that was a strong possibility. "So, Hank is definitely connected to Franklin and now possibly Anthony," Ethan remarked. "Ditto for Vernice. I suspect she visited Chloe a lot more often than she admitted, and that means she could have crossed paths with Hank and his sister."

"Totally agree," Grace said. "None of our three suspects get gold stars for being upfront and honest. But lies can be disproved, and that could lead to charges of obstruction and such. If I can arrest one of them, then that could give me some bargaining power. I want the SOB who killed Chloe put away before he or she strikes again."

Ethan wanted the same thing. So far, the killer hadn't come after Livvy, but that didn't mean they wouldn't. Anyone who saw her at the police station could have guessed that she was stunned and upset, and that could lead to speculation that her memory was returning.

That could make a killer anxious to silence her for good.

"And that brings me to my final update about Sunny," Grace said, yanking Ethan out of his thoughts. "Sunny's still being released, though it won't be until around six this evening since her doctor is waiting on some test results. I know the plan was for her to go to your place, but considering everything that's going on with Livvy and you, I can arrange a safe house for her."

"No," Livvy said. "She can come here."

Ethan wasn't so sure that was a good idea because Livvy did indeed have a lot going on, but so did Sunny. It might ease some of the stress for Sunny if she was with people she had already met instead of staying with whomever would be assigned to her at a safe house.

"Yes, bring Sunny here," he piped in.

"All right. Will do. And I'll let you know if there are any other updates. In the meantime, keep digging," Grace added before she said a quick goodbye and ended the call.

Ethan set his phone down and looked at Livvy. All of this was clearly taking a toll on her, so despite what she'd said earlier about falling apart if he touched her, he pulled her into his arms. She didn't back away. Just the opposite. She came off the stool where she'd been sitting, and she pressed herself against him.

"I'm so tired of all of this. The memory gaps are making things much worse," Livvy muttered. "In fact, if I could just remember, I might be able to say who the killer is."

Maybe her mother's killer, yes, but it was possible someone else had murdered Zadie and Chloe. So, getting her memory back might not give them what they needed to keep Sunny and her safe.

He eased away, met her gaze, and for some reason, he smiled. Despite everything, it warmed him to see her face. Livvy, his friend. That was first and foremost the basis of their relationship, and it had been that way for years. However, this extra level to it, this lovers' pull, felt good, too. And yeah, it still caused some guilt, but Ethan could feel that cooling just as the attraction was heating up.

"When this investigation is over, maybe we can go on a date," he suggested.

For a moment, she just looked stunned. Then, she smiled. "That's the third thing on the agenda after we catch a killer. That long talk you wanted. The gender reveal. And now a date. I'd love to go out with you," she tacked on.

Ethan's next breath was one of relief, and he risked touching his mouth to hers. Just the slightest of kisses. No more. Because more was only going to land them in bed and not working on the investigation.

"All right," she said, as if sensing they were about to go back into cop mode. "Back to Eden's list. And by now, some of the reports might be in from the CSIs."

"True, and I want to read the one from the spot where Sunny was attacked." The CSIs had found some shoeprints, and Ethan was eager to find out if they matched Hank's.

Or find out if they were dealing with someone else. Like Vernice or Anthony.

Livvy made a sound of agreement, and she pushed the rest of her salad aside and dragged over the laptop as she sat back on the barstool. "And I want to have another conversation with Sunny when she gets here. There's a reason Sunny's a target," she said. "Maybe because the killer thinks Zadie said something to her, but it could be more than that. It could be something that Sunny heard or saw."

Yeah, and that went right back to all their suspects.

Ethan grabbed his laptop, too, and he moved it next to Livvy's so they could work the list. They'd barely gotten started on that, though, when he heard something he hadn't been expecting.

A car engine.

Because he was nowhere on the route to and from town, he rarely got visitors, and with Livvy here, he didn't like the timing of anyone just showing up. That was why Ethan slid his hand over his gun as he made his way to the front window.

Livvy did the same thing, and she went with him to peer out at their visitor. The black Lexus that pulled to a stop in front of his house wasn't familiar, but the man who stepped out certainly was.

Franklin.

What the hell was he doing here?

Franklin fired some nervous glances around himself, and he tucked a manila folder under his arm before he started toward the porch.

"Stay back," Ethan muttered to Livvy.

He disengaged the security system only on the front door so he could open it a couple of inches. "What do you want?" Ethan snarled, and he made damn sure it was not a friendly greeting.

Franklin stopped in his tracks, eyeing Ethan's stance and gun. He swallowed hard. "I need to talk to Deputy Walsh. She's not at her house, so I figured she was here with you."

"How'd you get our addresses?" Ethan demanded.

He lifted his shoulder. "Renegade Canyon's a small town, and people talk."

Yeah, they did, but Ethan couldn't imagine something like that just coming up in random conversation. Franklin had likely sought out the information.

But why?

"What do you want?" he repeated.

This time Franklin sighed. Gone was the surliness that'd been present during the interview at the police station. Franklin looked exhausted. Maybe an act though, Ethan reminded himself.

"I have some things to tell Deputy Walsh. Livvy," he added in a barely audible whisper. "Things she'll want to know. We can talk out here," he said, still glancing around, "but it'd be better if I come in. I have something to give her."

"You're not coming in," Ethan was quick to tell him. "Whatever you have to say, you can say it there. Then, you can explain why you didn't bring it up when you were being questioned."

The man sighed again. "Because what I have to tell her is personal. It has nothing to do with Zadie's and my sister's murders."

Ethan doubted that. He figured anything to do with Franklin was also connected to the murders.

"What do you want to tell me?" Livvy asked, stepping into the doorway next to him. He had hoped she would stay to the side where she'd be better protected, but he understood her need to face this man head-on, too. Ethan would just need to stay vigilant in case this was some kind of ploy. Franklin could have come here to draw them out for a hired gun.

Or Franklin himself could plan on doing the killing.

He shifted his attention to Livvy, and Ethan wished he could read that expression on the doctor's face. It seemed to be a tangle of all sorts of emotions.

"Livvy," Franklin said, "I think you remembered something. I think that's why you left the interview. What did you remember?"

She huffed. "I thought you were here to tell me something, not ask questions that I won't answer."

He nodded as if he understood that. "I knew your mother," he blurted.

For only four words, they certainly packed a wallop. Ethan had to hand it to Livvy though. Other than a quick intake of breath, she didn't react. She just stood there and waited for Franklin to continue.

"At least I think it was your mother," he said. "I didn't realize it until I had a closer look at you and that sketch the sheriff showed me. That's when it all clicked for me. Her name was Belinda Anderson," he explained, "and she was a surrogate at New Hope."

"Belinda Anderson," Livvy muttered, no doubt testing it to see if it was familiar. She shook her head though. Obviously, it wasn't ringing any bells.

It didn't ring any bells for Ethan either, and he wished he could take out his phone and do a quick search of the woman. It was too risky, though, since he didn't trust Franklin. Added to that, all of this could be more lies.

"Was I one of the surrogate babies Belinda carried?" Livvy asked. "Am I your child?"

"No," the doctor answered. "No," he repeated, as if shocked by the questions. "You were four or five years old when Belinda came to New Hope. If I recall, she said a friend of a friend had referred her to New Hope and that she needed a place to stay with her little girl. With you," he emphasized. "But I don't remember your name."

"That makes two of us," she murmured. "Tell me about her. Was my father with her? And where is she now?"

Franklin scrubbed his hand over his face. "No, your father wasn't with her. I got the feeling she was running from something. Maybe him or an abusive relationship. Maybe she was just looking for a new start that the surrogacy money would give her. I'm afraid I don't know. In fact, I hadn't thought of Belinda in years until your sheriff showed me that sketch of her."

"And since you recognized it, why didn't you mention it then and there?" Ethan demanded.

"Because like I said, that doesn't have anything to do with now. Well, other than how this is affecting Livvy." He stopped, muttered some profanity. "As for where Belinda is…" His words trailed off. "I think I should start at the beginning."

"Do that," Ethan snapped. Still not offering up any niceties. And still not sure he was buying any of this. But with a name at least now Livvy might possibly have a starting point. She might finally learn who she was and what had happened when she was a child.

"Like I said," Franklin went on, and he wrapped his arms around himself and hunched against the cold wind, "Belinda came with you to New Hope, and after I examined her, I hired her for a gestational surrogacy. She lived at New Hope with you during the pregnancy."

He paused again and seemed to rethink what he'd been about to say. Ethan was certain the man was holding back on something. Maybe something important.

"The delivery went fine," he continued a moment later, "and Belinda asked if she could stay on for a while and maybe have another gestational surrogacy. We don't usually do back-to-backs like that, but I made an exception. I told her she could recover for six months and then she could carry another baby. Five months into that waiting period, she disappeared."

Beside him, he felt Livvy's arm tense. "With me?"

Franklin nodded but then stopped again. "Or so that's what Chloe told me," he amended.

Ethan felt the ice slide through his body, and it had nothing to do with the cold wind. "Chloe?" he questioned.

"Yes, when I asked where Belinda was, Chloe said she'd up and left with her daughter. And I believed her." Franklin's voice cracked a little. "I knew that Chloe didn't like Belinda. Paul was alive then, and she was jealous of the attention he was showing Belinda. So, I figured that Chloe had paid Belinda off or done something to convince her to leave."

Franklin squeezed his eyes shut a moment and groaned before he took the manila envelope from beneath his arm. Extending it out to them, Franklin walked to the porch steps. His movements were slow and cautious. No sudden moves to make them think he could be going for a gun. As soon as Livvy took the envelope, Franklin went back into the yard.

The envelope was at least two inches thick, and when Livvy opened it, Ethan saw it was some paper, some of which had been photocopied. There were also two old cassette tapes.

"I'm sure you'll want to look through all of that," Franklin explained, "but I can give you the broad strokes now. Let me say first, though, that I'm so very sorry for what Chloe did."

That ice inside Ethan went up a notch. "What did she do?" he asked.

Franklin tipped his head to the envelope. "It's all in there, a mix of memos and recordings of conversations and meetings." He dragged in a long breath. "I didn't know it at the time, but a few weeks after Belinda and her daughter disappeared, Hank Stover started blackmailing Chloe. Some of his notes are in there."

"Blackmailing her for what?" Ethan asked, though he was pretty sure he knew where this was going.

The doctor swallowed hard. "For murdering Belinda."

And there it was. Maybe a lie. But this felt like the cold, hard truth.

"I didn't find that file until after you came to New Hope and told us that Zadie was dead," Franklin continued. "Chloe said something after you left. Something about how the past should just die, so when she went to San Antonio for a meeting, I searched her office. I didn't ransack it," he insisted. "And I didn't kill her."

Again, Ethan had no idea if that was true, and at the moment, he didn't care. He needed to hear what'd happened to Livvy's mother.

"After you found the file, you read it and listened to the recordings?" he prompted.

Franklin nodded. "And it took me a while to make sense of it. Then, I realized Hank had tried to blackmail her. The details were all there. Chloe had gotten enraged when she believed Belinda had slept with Paul."

"Did she?" Livvy asked.

"I don't know. I don't think so, but Chloe wasn't always rational when it came to Paul. Anyway, on the recording, Chloe admits she put on surgical gloves, grabbed a knife and went after Belinda when she ran away with you. Unbeknownst to Chloe, Hank was at New Hope visiting his sister, and he followed all three of you. He saw Chloe confront Belinda at the old house. And saw Chloe kill her."

Hell. Ethan could see it all playing out. The murder that had become Livvy's nightmare.

"Chloe stabbed Belinda multiple times," Franklin went on. "And put her in the bathtub."

Livvy made a soft sound—part groan, part sob. "Where was I during all of this?" she asked.

He glanced away for a moment. "According to what Chloe said on the recording, you were there. You tried to take the knife from her, but she pushed you. You fell, hit your head and went unconscious. Chloe admitted to Hank later that she took the knife because she knew it would have your prints on it and not hers."

"Why not just kill me?" Livvy asked. "I was a witness."

The doctor looked her straight in the eyes. “I don’t know. Maybe she couldn’t kill a child. Maybe she decided to take her chances that no one would believe you if you told anyone what you’d seen.”

Ethan considered that. Yeah, that was possible. And Chloe could have possibly disposed of the body and cleaned up the blood after Livvy left. That way, if Livvy did indeed lead the police back to the house, there’d be no proof that a murder had happened.

“So, how the hell did the knife end up with my ex-mother-in-law?” he demanded.

Franklin looked genuinely surprised by the question. “I guess Chloe must have sent it to her.”

Ethan couldn’t think of a reason for Chloe to do that unless she wanted to muddy the waters of the investigation into Zadie’s death.

“Did Chloe kill Zadie, too?” Livvy asked.

“I don’t know. Maybe,” Franklin admitted. “Probably,” he amended. “I found that file in the storage room off Chloe’s office. The file folder was sticking up a little, as if someone had recently pulled it out. Zadie could have done that.”

Yeah. And it could have given Chloe motive to hire Hank to kill her. *Could have*. But again, Ethan didn’t intend to take Franklin’s word for it.

“Why did Chloe keep this file since it supposedly incriminates her for murder?” Ethan asked.

“From what I can tell, it was some kind of insurance. Chloe paid Hank some hush money but then told him if he came back for more that his blackmail note and what he said on the recording could make him an accessory after the fact for murder. He’d be arrested, too.”

So, Chloe and Hank had made a pact to hide the truth.

To hide a murder. And Livvy had become collateral damage. Heck, so had Zadie and Sunny.

"For what it's worth, I don't believe this was the first time my sister killed someone in a jealous rage," Franklin went on. "Look into the death of a woman named Ivy Milbrath. I think she had something to do with that."

Anthony's mother. Oh, they would look more all right. But first, Ethan had to stop all of this from crushing Livvy. He could feel the panic and dread coming off her in hot waves.

Franklin must have noticed it, too. "I'm sorry for the damage my sister did," he repeated, heading back to his car. "So very sorry."

Ethan didn't waste any time. He eased Livvy back inside, shut the door, locked it and reengaged the security. He'd barely turned toward her before she all but collapsed into his arms.

# *Chapter Fifteen*

Livvy sat at the kitchen counter, listening to the phone conversation that Grace was having with the lab. It was the second time the sheriff had been on the line with them since she'd arrived at Ethan's house about an hour earlier.

An arrival brought on by Ethan's call to let her know what had happened.

And what had happened was a lot.

Livvy was still reeling from everything that Franklin had told them, and it felt as if she was mentally wading through thick, sticky mud. There were so many thoughts coming at her. Broken bits of memories, too, and it was hard to sort everything out. But sorting and dealing were going to have to happen.

And fast.

Because if everything Franklin had told them turned out to be true, then what had happened twenty-eight years ago could be the reason Chloe and Zadie were dead.

That was why Grace was on the phone, trying to get info on the lab from the file she'd had a courier pick up. She was especially interested to learn if the recordings were the real deal or something that had been faked with AI or spliced together from other recordings. Because knowing that could determine if Franklin had put it together to cast blame on his sister while also trying to make himself look innocent of murder.

Before the lab courier had picked up the file, Ethan had made copies of everything, and he was now seated across from her, listening to one of the recordings through an earbud. He'd likely chosen to review it that way so he could spare Livvy having to hear Chloe plotting murder.

Drawing in a long breath, Livvy forced her attention back to the laptop in front of her, the one with what seemed to be an endless search for a woman named Belinda Anderson. There were over two hundred possibilities in the databases, and so far none of them were panning out to have possibly been her mother.

Her *dead* mother.

Who Chloe had supposedly killed.

As sickening as that possibility was, Livvy wished she could remember. Not just fragments but the entire hellish ordeal. That way she would know what was true. That way she would know if she was this Belinda Anderson's daughter.

She glanced up and saw that Ethan was looking at her. Studying her. No doubt checking to see if she was on the verge of falling apart. Again. That'd happened right after Franklin had left. Her legs had simply given way. Her breath had vanished. And her heart had felt ready to beat right out of her chest.

Ethan had held her. Soothed her. And leveled her out enough for him to call Grace. At the time, Livvy hadn't wanted that, hadn't wanted the sheriff to see her in this emotional muddle. But it'd been the right thing to do because now they were focused on the investigation.

"Thanks," Livvy heard Grace say to the person on the other end of her phone line.

Ethan hit Pause on the recording, and Livvy and he shifted their attention to Grace.

"The recordings are legit," she relayed to them. She pinned her gaze to Ethan. "Are you getting anything from them?"

He nodded. "So far, it's just as Franklin said. Chloe was jealous of Belinda and went after her. Hank saw what went on, blackmailed her, and Chloe kept the file as leverage over him." Ethan huffed. "What I can't figure out is why Chloe didn't lock the file away instead of shelving it with her other records."

"Sunny might be able to help with that," Grace said, surprising them.

"The lab IDed multiple sets of prints on the folder. Ethan's and yours, of course. Zadie's and Chloe's, since theirs are now on file. An unidentified set that no doubt belongs to Franklin." She paused. "And Sunny's."

"Sunny's?" Livvy questioned. "Why were her prints on the folder? And in the database?"

"She gave them voluntarily earlier today when I told her we needed them for elimination purposes to help the CSIs who were processing the crime scene at New Hope." Grace shrugged. "Of course, her prints could have gotten on the folder just because she handled it, not knowing what it was. But the tech believes Sunny's and Zadie's are the most recent ones. Theirs and a third set that probably belongs to Franklin."

Livvy considered all of that. Sunny certainly hadn't mentioned a file like that, and it seemed as if she would have.

"Trust me, I'll be asking Sunny about this when I pick her up soon." Grace checked the time. "And FYI, I'll be taking her to my place. There's good security there, and you two have enough to deal with right now."

Livvy couldn't argue that, though she did want to talk to Sunny. Not only about the contents of that file but any gossip that Sunny might have heard about Chloe's violent streak. It was possible that Chloe had run-ins with other women about Paul, and if so, they might have info. If they were alive, that is.

"Sunny also asked if tomorrow morning I could take her to the house where her sister's body was found," Grace continued. "I reluctantly agreed," she muttered, not sounding especially pleased about that. "It hasn't been cleaned yet, which means Zadie's blood is still there."

"The house needs to be processed for old blood," Livvy blurted. "For my…mother's," she managed to say. The word felt as if it'd gotten stuck in her throat.

Grace sighed, nodded. "That's being done as we speak. And the CSIs should be done in a couple of hours. If they turn up anything, they'll let us know."

Finding blood or DNA that old was a serious long shot, but it was possible some blood had seeped into the old wood floor and had gotten trapped there.

"I want to see the house, too," Livvy said.

And that got instant headshakes and disapproving groans from both Grace and Ethan.

"It might trigger my memory," she argued before Grace could flat-out refuse. "And if I remember something, then it could give us a clearer picture of who murdered Chloe."

They didn't dispute that. Couldn't. But Livvy saw the concern in their eyes. She was feeling a whole lot of concern, too, but this might be the fastest way to recover her memory and catch a killer.

"It's time I remembered," Livvy added.

The seconds crawled by. And crawled. Before Grace muttered some profanity and nodded. "All right, you can go there in the morning with Sunny and me. You, too," she added to Ethan, "since I know you want to be there for Livvy."

"I do," he was quick to verify.

"Tomorrow morning at eight, then," Grace decided. "Meet us there, and maybe we'll get a break." She tipped her head to Livvy's laptop. "Speaking of breaks, anything yet on our Belinda Anderson?"

Livvy was about to say no, but when she looked at the screen, she saw the last entry, and something about it jumped right out at her. Thirty-one years ago, a Belinda Tate Anderson had testified against her husband, Quentin, in a case of felony domestic violence.

"Maybe," Livvy heard herself say.

She sat back down on the barstool, her fingers moving quickly now on the keyboard to pull up the file. Ethan and Grace must have realized that she was onto something because they moved in closer so they could see the screen.

And the info loaded.

The picture popped up first. One from an old driver's license. Livvy felt the slam of emotions. The shock, the grief, the unbearable sadness all rolled into one.

Because that was the face of the dead woman, the one from her nightmares.

Livvy couldn't look at the picture for long, not with the reaction it was causing inside her. She had to focus. Had to keep reading. And she saw that nearly thirty years ago to the day, Belinda had testified against her husband in a San Antonio trial that had resulted in his conviction for felony domestic violence. Since it'd been his third conviction, he had been sentenced to ten years.

Livvy kept scrolling, moving to the background info on Belinda Tate Anderson. Born fifty-seven years ago in Houston, where she was orphaned at age sixteen when both of her parents were killed in a car crash. And the irony of that? Livvy saw that Belinda had spent the next year and a half in the foster care system. Much less time than Livvy but still the same system.

"No criminal record," Ethan read aloud. "Married to Quentin when she was twenty-one, and two years later, she had a child, Alyssa."

"Alyssa," Livvy repeated.

After a couple of deep breaths, she kept on scrolling, only to realize there wasn't anything else after the trial. That was it. No driver's license renewal. No cyber footprint left of any kind.

"That's when she went to New Hope," Livvy concluded. "And after she disappeared, there was no missing person's report ever filed."

If Franklin was to be believed, Chloe had told him that Belinda had simply left. Of course, she hadn't left by choice, and if Chloe had indeed murdered her, there was no way she would have told the police she was missing.

"What about her husband, Quentin?" Grace asked.

Livvy shifted the search, wondering if he could have played a part in Belinda's death. But she soon dismissed that. Less than a year after he'd gone to prison for the felony domestic abuse charge, Quentin Anderson had been killed in a fight with several other inmates.

So, both of her parents were dead. And while Livvy was actually thankful that Quentin wasn't in the picture, she felt the loss of her mother bone deep. It crushed her heart to think of the hell Belinda had gone through with her husband only to end up being murdered.

"This is her," she said. "This is the right one."

Neither Grace nor Ethan disputed that. Grace put her hand on Livvy's shoulder and gave it a gentle squeeze. "I'm sorry," she muttered.

The silence hung there for a while, not nearly long enough for Livvy to try to grasp everything she'd just read, but Grace and Ethan gave her some time to tamp down the worst of the sensations. The senseless loss for both Belinda and her.

Grace cleared her throat and checked the time again. "I have to go pick up Sunny, but if you need anything, just let me know."

Livvy managed a nod and was thankful that she didn't have to get to her feet. Ethan showed Grace to the door, and after he locked up, he made his way back to her. He didn't even glance at the info on the computer screen. He simply scooped her up in his arms and started walking.

She didn't protest. Couldn't. Livvy just let him carry her into the guest bathroom where he turned on the water in the tub. "Take a long soak," he suggested.

Livvy doubted that was going to fix things, but she thought of something that might help. She took hold of Ethan and pulled him into her arms. Yes, it was a huge risk with her emotions running so high, but she needed him to hold her.

And he did.

Performing his usual magic, he gathered her close, pressing against her. They sank down onto the floor, Ethan anchoring his back against the tub, and he let go of her only long enough to turn off the water.

"I don't feel like an Alyssa," she muttered. "I feel like Livvy."

He brushed a kiss on the top of her head. "Because you are Livvy and have been for twenty-eight years."

She knew that but had apparently needed to hear it because it lifted some of the weight from her heart. Of course, a lot of that heaviness would likely be there for a long time. Livvy knew she wouldn't be able to quickly process what she'd learned and handle the grief for her dead mother. No, that would have to come bit by bit.

And she'd need more information.

A deeper background check might help with that so she could learn about her mother's family. It was possible she had other relatives out there. Not that she wanted to deal with that now, but she might down the road.

"About the visit to the house tomorrow," he said, his words dripping with concern. "Are you sure you don't want to give that a day or two?"

"I do want that," she agreed, "but more than that, I have to know what happened. Right now, all I have is Chloe's file and Franklin's account of things. Neither of which might be the total truth."

He sighed, causing her to look up at him. Oh, yes, the worry and concern were definitely there and had darkened his gray eyes to the color of a storm cloud.

"Just think about this investigation being over," she said. "Being solved. A killer identified and caught. Then, we can go on that date."

As she'd hoped, that caused him to smile. Even though it was barely there, it did amazing things to his face. Then again, Ethan's face hit the *amazing* mark without him doing anything at all.

Livvy didn't try to talk herself out of what she was about to do. She kissed him. And yes, that helped, too. It wasn't going to undo any of the bad stuff that'd happened, but for this moment, the kiss did the job.

Of course, since the kiss was with Ethan, it did more than just level out some of the tension. It generated some heat, and that was a nice bonus. So was the sound of her name that he whispered against her mouth.

"Livvy."

He seemed to be saying it as a warning, that they were playing with fire. And they were. No doubts about that. But it didn't stop Livvy. In fact, she turned, easing onto his lap so she could press against him and deepen the kiss.

Her body very much approved of this new contact, and the heat slipped up a notch. It was obviously doing the same to Ethan, too, because she felt no hesitation in him now. Just the opposite. He hooked his arm around her, dragging her even closer until they were fitted against each other as much as her baby bump would allow.

The kiss got hotter. Hungrier. Filled with so much need, and the need, of course, fueled the urgency. A great kiss could do that—amp up things from foreplay to a raging hunger that was already demanding things.

Like more kisses.

More contact. More everything.

Livvy sated the need by touching Ethan. Not some frantic rush to take in everything at once. Not yet anyway. She kept it slow, her palm gliding over his chest, over all those muscles.

Then, to his stomach.

Plenty of muscles there, too, and when she went even lower, when her hand slid over the front of his jeans, she felt the hard length of him.

He made a ragged sound of pleasure and caught onto her shoulder, breaking the kiss so they could make eye contact.

"We need to rethink this," he managed to say, though it was obvious he was having trouble getting out the words.

Yes, they probably did. But Livvy didn't want to do any more thinking right now. She only wanted Ethan and the comfort—and the pleasure he could give her.

"It's okay," she said, trying to reassure him.

She needed no such reassurances for herself. Livvy knew exactly what she wanted, and that was why she kissed him again. No slow, exploring pace now. This kiss was scalding hot and filled with fire and hunger. A good combination for skipping past a couple of levels of foreplay.

And that was what Livvy did.

She somehow managed to remove his shoulder holster. Then, his shirt. And she got an amazing reward for that. Now when she touched him, it was skin to skin. No barrier of clothes, and it made her want so much more.

Apparently, it did the same for Ethan because he, too, rid her of her holster and shirt. He didn't waste any time, kissing the tops of her breasts. Long, lingering caresses of his mouth that escalated big time when he shoved down the cups of her bra and gave some kisses that shot the heat through the roof.

And through every inch of her body.

Mercy, she wanted him, and it had to be now.

She was glad that Ethan was on the same page with her about that, and the battle started for them to get rid of the rest of their clothes. It wasn't easy since the need had pushed this into frantic mode.

Ethan yanked off her bra and went after her pants. She went after his belt and jeans, and throughout all of it, they continued to kiss and touch. Continued to fuel the fire that was already burning out of control.

But Ethan seemed to find some control just as they got

naked. Livvy could feel him battling the need. Trying to be gentle as he pulled her back onto her lap.

She was glad he hadn't tried to move this into the bedroom. Livvy didn't want to wait even that handful of seconds to have him, and the moment she was straddling him, she took him inside her.

And the pleasure erupted through her.

Wonderful pleasure that robbed her of her breath. Everything though was at the highest level. The sensations of him being inside her. Of pushing into her.

The need just kept on growing though with each long, hard stroke. And while part of her wanted to savor this, to hold on to these moments, Livvy knew that wasn't going to happen.

No.

Their bodies were calling the shots here, and the demanding need was skyrocketing until Livvy knew she couldn't hold on much longer.

And she didn't.

She just let Ethan take her higher, higher, higher. To the only place she wanted to go. To that peak. Then, to the release.

The climax came, rippling through her. Giving her a final burst of that pleasure. Ethan wasn't far behind her. He gathered her in his arms and surrendered right along with her.

# *Chapter Sixteen*

As he watched Livvy eat her breakfast, Ethan was feeling a lot of things. Worry over the investigation. Over the possibility of Livvy being emotionally crushed if her memory did fully return. Heck, he was even concerned about the safety of the baby and her.

One thing he wasn't feeling was regret.

It had no doubt muddied their relationship waters for them to have sex, again, but he was having a hard time being sorry about it happening. Along with it being pretty damn amazing, Livvy had seemed to relax. And later, she'd fallen asleep in his arms.

No nightmare.

That was somewhat of a miracle, considering the hell she'd been through for the past two days. Of course, the "hell" wasn't finished. Ethan knew that soon reports would be coming in on Belinda and the two crime scenes. Added to that, a second investigation would need to be opened on her mother.

All of that would no doubt be like adding salt to Livvy's wounds, but for now, for this moment, she seemed, well, settled while she ate the eggs and toast he'd made for her.

She wasn't noticing that he was studying her because she had her attention on her laptop screen where she was reading a transcript of the recordings that had been in the file Franklin had given them. It had to be hard to read about Chloe plotting Belinda's murder, but he wasn't seeing that on her face. Maybe she was looking at the info as simply evidence needed to solve a case. If so, he hoped she could keep that attitude for a while longer until they had caught the killer.

"I'm all right," she said, glancing up at him. So, she'd noticed him studying her after all. "How about you?"

Ethan felt himself smile, and to answer her, he leaned in and dropped a kiss onto her mouth. He expected her to return the smile.

She didn't.

Instead, she sighed. "We really do need to have that talk, don't we?"

His stomach went into a knot. He definitely didn't like the sound of that. "Are you dumping me?" he had to ask.

Judging from her face—mouth dropping open and eyes widening—he'd thankfully gotten that wrong. "No, uh, I was thinking more along the lines of asking you just how hard should I be guarding my heart."

Now it was his turn to look surprised. He had no idea how to respond to that and didn't get the chance anyway because Livvy continued.

"I shouldn't be saying this, but I'm in love with you," she blurted, and she looked stunned and a little horrified at her confession. "And no, it doesn't have to do with the great sex. That's just...icing. It doesn't have to do with the baby either. That's more icing." She stopped, groaned. "I'm babbling. Sorry—forget everything I just said."

Not a chance. In fact, Ethan was certain he'd remember that for the rest of his life. He was also equally certain that it scared the devil out of him. He wasn't ready to fall in love again.

Was he?

If he loved anyone again, it would definitely be Livvy, but…hell in a handbasket, his mind was all muddled now, and even though she'd said her feelings for him had nothing to do with the baby, or the great sex, that was all part of this.

Wasn't it?

Ethan did a whole lot of mental cursing, and he actually felt a little reprieve when Livvy's phone rang. He needed a couple of seconds to tamp down the whirlwind in his head. A couple of seconds to catch his breath.

Livvy was in love with him.

And he had to figure out what to do about that.

She kept her gaze on him until she picked up her phone. "It's Grace," she relayed to him.

Unlike what Livvy had just said, the call was expected. The night before Grace had texted to let them know she'd picked up Sunny from the hospital but that she wouldn't be talking to the woman about her fingerprints on the file until morning. She'd decided to let Sunny try to get a good night's sleep before discussing that with her.

"How's everything there this morning?" Grace greeted after Livvy answered the call and put it on speaker.

"Fine," they said in unison.

A little too fast. And more than just a little tense. Damn it. He'd blown it, and Ethan didn't know how to fix it.

"Okay," Grace replied as if she hadn't bought their response. "Well, I just wanted you to know that the CSIs did finish up inside at the old house. They're still examining the area around it, but we've been cleared to visit the scene, so Sunny and I are about to head out there in a couple of minutes. Do you still want to join us?"

"Yes," Livvy said, already standing.

Both Grace and Ethan sighed. "All right," Grace muttered. "FYI, you'll want to hear what she has to say about her fingerprints being on that file. It doesn't really give us a break in the case, just more of an insight. See you in about twenty minutes," she tacked on before ending the call.

"Insight," Ethan repeated.

He was all for that. All for Livvy and him having an air clearing, too, but he decided to wait until they were back here for that.

They put on their shoulder holsters, and since Ethan had put the cruiser in the garage, they headed there, making their way through the mudroom, where they grabbed their coats.

When Livvy pulled out of the garage, it was as if they'd been plunged right into winter. Of course, Ethan had already seen the dark skies from the windows, and he had known they wouldn't have a warm, sunny morning for this visit, but it looked as if they were on the verge of getting some ice or snow. Because the old house didn't have heat, maybe that would shorten this visit. Ethan wanted Livvy to spend as little time there as possible, only long enough to get whatever answers she hoped to get.

They had barely made it out of the driveway when both of their phones dinged with texts, and the head county CSI's name flashed on the dash monitor. Since it was a group message to the sheriff and all the deputies, Ethan figured it was one of the many reports and updates that would be coming in. And it was. But this was an update that might give Livvy a jolt.

"They found old blood under the floorboards in the

bathroom," he read aloud. "Significant amounts of it, and samples are being sent for testing."

So, that was likely the proof that Livvy's mother had indeed been murdered there, and he glanced at her to see how she was handling that. He was surprised when he saw her nod.

"Good," she murmured. "This might mean we're one step closer to learning the whole truth about what happened."

True. But that didn't mean the lab would be able to prove the blood was Belinda's. By now, any components of the blood, including the DNA, would likely be degraded. Still, if they could narrow down the timing of how long it'd been there, that would add to the details they already had.

When Livvy took the final turn onto the road to the house, Ethan spotted Grace's cruiser. And Grace herself. Sunny and she were standing in front of the house, and their shoulders were hunched, no doubt to shield themselves against the bitter chill.

Livvy parked behind them, and they got out as well. Yeah, it was definitely cold, and the wind was slashing through the bare tree limbs and the cornstalks that looked like something straight out of a horror movie. It only added to that knot that was still in Ethan's stomach.

"Sunny," Livvy greeted.

The woman nodded, but there was nothing cheerful about it. She glanced at the house as if both dreading this but also determined to go through with it. Like Livvy, Sunny probably thought she'd find answers here. Ethan hoped that was all they found, and the uneasiness went up a notch.

"Let's talk inside," Grace said, leading them up the rickety porch steps and into the front room.

Sunny glanced around before her attention landed on the narrow hall. Even though some of the wall was missing, it wasn't possible to see into the bathroom, but she no doubt knew it was in that direction.

Livvy was doing her own glancing around as well, and it was probably a toss-up between Sunny and her as to which one was having the harder time by being here. Both had had family die in this miserable place. Or at least it'd been where their bodies had been dumped.

"Before we take a look at the bathroom," Grace said, getting their attention, "Sunny has some things she wants to tell you."

The dread on Sunny's face escalated a whole bunch, but she nodded. "It's about the file Grace said Franklin gave you." She paused, clamping her teeth over her bottom lip for a moment. "Zadie showed me the file. That's why my fingerprints were on it."

"She showed it to you?" Livvy questioned. "When?"

Sunny dragged in a long breath. "It was about two months ago. Zadie brought it to my quarters one night. She said that Chloe had left her safe open, and Zadie spotted the folder. There was enough of the old cassette tape sticking out to make her curious, so she had a look." Another pause. "Zadie told me that Chloe had done something very bad. Something that could get her locked away in prison for a long time."

Yeah, if the contents of that file were true, Chloe could have been looking at the death penalty.

"Did she say what exactly Chloe had done, or did you read the file for yourself?" Ethan asked.

Sunny was quick to shake her head. "No to both of those. In fact, I told Zadie to put the file back and forget that she'd ever seen it. I know that sounds wrong—

cowardly, even—but I reminded her that whatever was in there might not even be about Chloe but a patient."

Ethan didn't think Sunny was lying about that. No need. And Chloe could indeed have put sensitive patient info in that safe.

"And how did Zadie react to what you told her?" Livvy pressed when Sunny fell silent.

"She agreed with me, eventually, but when she tried to return it, Chloe had already locked the safe. Zadie didn't have the combination and she didn't want Chloe to know she'd taken it, so she slipped it in with the rest of the files in the records room. She intended to put it back in the safe when she got the chance. But she never got that chance." Sunny's voice broke, and tears pooled in her eyes. "Grace said that Franklin had found it."

Ethan nodded. Franklin had said that, but they had no idea if it was true, that he'd simply pulled it from the shelf. If he'd been the one to ransack Chloe's office, he could have gotten it then.

"Any idea if Zadie showed the file to anyone else?" Livvy wanted to know. "Like Anthony, for instance? Or Vernice, the woman who visited Chloe at New Hope? Or maybe she even showed it to Franklin or someone else on the staff who would have told Franklin about it?"

Sunny's eyes suddenly went wide. "I don't think Zadie said anything about the file to any of them. At least she didn't mention doing that." She pressed her trembling fingers to her mouth. "Oh, God. Is that why Zadie was murdered? Because she showed it to someone?"

"It's possible," Ethan had to admit.

She gasped. "But why would one of them have killed her because of that file? What was in there that would make someone do that?"

Both good questions. And it went right back to their three suspects. Anthony had only been ten years old at the time of Belinda's death, but he certainly could have been the one to kill Zadie and Chloe. And Anthony admitted that he hooked up with Zadie because he wanted to prove that Chloe had killed his mother.

As for Franklin or Vernice, either of them could have wanted to silence Zadie if she'd learned about Belinda's murder because it could possibly implicate them as accessories after the fact. Heck, even accomplices if one of them had actually helped Chloe in any way.

"I should have insisted that Zadie take the file to the police," Sunny went on. "If I had, she might still be alive."

That was possible, but Zadie could have sealed her fate simply by learning the info that had been in the file. If Chloe had realized it was missing, she could have figured out Zadie had taken it and killed her to make sure she never said a word about it to anyone. Adding to that, it could have been Chloe herself who'd ransacked her office if she'd realized the file wasn't in the safe.

Of course, that didn't give them a clear answer as to who'd murdered Chloe.

"Ready to go look in the bathroom?" Grace asked, the sound of her voice blending with the wind howling through the cracks in the house.

Both Livvy and Sunny nodded, and Grace led the way. Ethan glanced around, looking for anything the CSIs might have missed. Looking, too, to try to see the place through the eyes of a killer.

And through Livvy's.

Because she had almost certainly been here. Had likely seen horrible things that were still feeding her nightmares all these years later.

Grace stepped into the bathroom, moving to the side to give Livvy and Sunny a clear view of the tub. Ethan hung back a little but stayed close enough in case Livvy needed him.

"Was Zadie killed here?" Sunny asked, her voice as unsteady as she looked. She was shivering, and Ethan figured it was from the cold.

"We believe so," Grace said.

Ethan had read the ME's report just an hour ago, and he believed that someone had hit Zadie on the head, probably rendering her unconscious before putting her in the tub, undressing her and then stabbing her to death.

Any of their suspects could have murdered using that method. Zadie hadn't been a large woman, but it didn't seem likely that Vernice or Chloe could have dragged her into the tub. Anthony, however, could have lifted her.

What the ME's report hadn't been able to tell them was why the killer had staged this.

If it was to implicate Livvy or to mentally terrorize her by recreating her nightmare, then it pointed to Vernice or Chloe being the culprit. But if Anthony had seen the contents of that file, if Zadie had shown it to him, then he would have known about Belinda's body being left in this very tub.

Livvy made an odd sound that had Ethan's gaze firing to her. She was looking at him, and he could see in her eyes that something was wrong.

"What is it?" he asked, automatically looking at her baby bump.

But she didn't have her hand over her stomach, and that wasn't a look of pain on her face. She fluttered her hands to the window but didn't say anything. Livvy just hurried past Grace and Sunny.

Out of the room.

And into his arms.

"I remembered something," she whispered, though her voice had hardly any sound.

Hell. Whatever it was, it couldn't be good. Livvy was trembling all over, and she took hold of him to drag him away from the room.

"Outside," Livvy said, moving back enough to take his hand and get them moving.

She didn't head for the front door but instead took the one off the kitchen. There was no actual door here, just a gaping hole that led to what had once been a porch. Now it was just old boards lying on the ground.

"Here," she insisted, leading him to the small window outside the bathroom. Sunny and Grace were no longer there. They'd no doubt come outside to see what was going on with her.

"I saw her here that night," Livvy went on. Her eyes had a glazed look to them now. Trapped in the past. In the nightmare. "She was at the window. And she must have seen when Chloe stabbed my mother."

Livvy stopped, stared up at him, and a raw sob tore from her throat. "Oh, God. Chloe killed my mother, Ethan. She stabbed her, and my mother was screaming and bleeding. But Chloe just kept stabbing her, and then she shoved her into the tub."

Ethan silently cursed, and he hauled Livvy to him, trying to protect her from…everything. And failing big time. He couldn't undo the past, but he sure as hell could help her deal with the fallout.

Grace and Sunny came out into the backyard, both of them clearly puzzled as to what was going on. Neither of them said anything though. Probably because Livvy looked ready to fall apart. But there was something that Ethan had to know. He had to hear Livvy spell it out.

"Who was at the window?" he asked, already dreading the answer.

"Vernice," Livvy muttered. "It was Vernice." She blinked back tears. "I remember it all, Ethan. I remember everything."

He pulled her back to him and got her moving toward the cruiser. "I need to get her out of here," he insisted.

Grace didn't argue, and Sunny and she followed them toward the front of the house. They didn't get far though. Only a couple of steps. Before all hell broke loose.

There was the blast of a gunshot. Loud and deafening. Followed by a scream of pain.

# *Chapter Seventeen*

Livvy heard the sound and knew exactly what had happened. Someone had fired a shot at them.

And Sunny had no doubt been hit.

That scream was one of intense pain.

Drawing her gun, Livvy whirled around and saw the blood already spreading over the shoulder of Sunny's camel-colored coat. Yes, she'd been shot. Maybe not a fatal wound. Not yet anyway. But the shooter obviously wasn't done.

In a blink, another shot rang out just as Grace hooked her arm around Sunny and dragged her to the ground. She didn't stop there. Grace pulled her behind some weed-filled shrubs. Not much cover, and it was obvious Sunny was the target since a third shot went in her direction.

Livvy and Ethan got moving, too. They scrambled behind the meager cover of a toppled front-porch railing. No way would it protect them from bullets. Ditto for where Sunny and Grace were. And that meant they had to spot the shooter and stop him or her now before the worst happened.

Before someone got killed.

She thought of her baby. Of the risk and danger that her precious child was in. Ethan was no doubt doing the same because he positioned himself in front of her. Protecting them. Livvy was thankful for that, but at the same time, she was terrified for him. After all, they were only a few feet from Sunny, and the shooter might decide to take them all out.

The cruisers were parked to their right and were too far away for them to reach. Trying to get to them would make them easy to pick off, especially since Sunny probably wouldn't be able to move fast enough.

More shots came, slamming into the ground right by Sunny and Grace. Sunny screamed again, and Livvy prayed she hadn't been hit a second time. Prayed, too, that they'd all make it out of this alive, away from this hellish place where two women had already died.

But who was doing this? Who was shooting at them?

Livvy hoped she got the chance to learn the answer to that, and maybe then they could make an arrest and get some justice for Zadie.

She heard Grace murmuring something and realized she was calling for an ambulance and backup. Good. Sunny would need to get to the hospital, and they could use help stopping the shooter. The problem with that was the ambulance wouldn't be able to approach the house as long as there was active gunfire.

And there was plenty of that.

There were two more shots, and Livvy used the sound of it to try to pinpoint their attacker. The wind and Sunny's screams weren't helping with that. Ditto for her own gusting breath and pounding pulse. Her teeth were chattering as well from the cold. But when there was another blast from a gunshot, Livvy whirled in the direction of the cornfield.

She was certain the shooter was in there, but from her

angle she couldn't see who was doing this. Apparently, neither could Ethan because he levered himself up a little. Just as a bullet slammed into the house right next to them. Livvy took hold of his shoulder and hauled him back down.

"See anyone?" Grace asked.

"No," Livvy and Ethan said in unison.

It was Ethan who added, "But I think the shooter is at my ten o'clock."

Livvy thought that as well, and what she wanted to do was to send some shots of her own in that direction. But it would be a huge risk to do that since the shots could end up hitting someone traveling on the road. There was also the possibility that if they did aim at the shooter, then he or she would just move farther to the left and take up cover behind the bulletproof cruisers.

Sunny finally stopped screaming, the sound of her voice trailing off into a whimpering sob. She had to be terrified, not just of being killed but bleeding out right here where her sister had died. Maybe her injuries weren't life-threatening, and the ambulance would be able to get to her in time.

Two more shots came, and these hadn't been aimed at Sunny but at Ethan and her. So, now they were the targets, too.

Of course they were.

The shooter obviously didn't want to leave any potential witnesses behind. Too bad they hadn't actually seen anything to help them identify the person who was doing this. That way at least she might know exactly why they were all in danger.

"How's Sunny doing?" Livvy muttered to Grace when there was a lull in the shooting.

"I think I've gotten the blood flow slowed down some," Grace replied.

Livvy glanced over at them, and while she couldn't see Sunny because of Grace being in front of her, Grace was no longer wearing her jacket. She'd likely pulled it off to use as a compress on the wound.

"I'm going to have Sunny crawl under the house," Grace let them know. "Livvy, I want you to do the same. Think of the baby," she added, knowing that saying that was more effective than giving an outright order.

Livvy peered behind her at the narrow opening beneath the house. Only about a foot high, which meant she'd have to squeeze underneath it. It would definitely get her out of the direct line of fire, but she didn't want to think of all the critters lurking there.

From the corner of her eye, Livvy saw Grace maneuvering Sunny through that narrow opening. And yes, she saw the blood now, too. Maybe Grace had indeed managed to staunch it some, but Sunny was definitely still at risk of bleeding out. They needed to put an end to this now.

"What if we fire shots into the ground of the cornfield?" Livvy asked. "We could keep our aims low so there's no risk of hitting anyone who might be driving by on the nearby road."

Grace volleyed glances at both the cornfield and the direction of the road, and after a few moments of thought, she nodded. "Maybe it'll hit the SOB, and if not, it might at least send him or her running."

That was the idea, and while Livvy didn't relish their attacker escaping, it would be the first step in getting Sunny the help she needed.

"All right, Ethan and you fire," Grace instructed. She couldn't do the same without moving out into the open.

Livvy and Ethan took aim to do just that. But there was movement in the field. Someone was running toward them, shoving the cornstalks aside. If this was the shooter, then this wasn't an attempt to escape. It was more like a last-ditch effort to take them out while knowing he or she would be gunned down.

But Livvy didn't intend for them to be taken out.

She held off shooting. Ethan did as well. And they kept their weapons aimed at those moving stalks.

Finally, someone burst through them, and Livvy stopped herself from pulling the trigger when she saw the woman.

Vernice.

Not armed. Or at least not holding a gun. That was because her hands were duct-taped together at the wrists in front of her. There was also a swath of the tape across her mouth. Her eyes were wild, terrified. And while the woman appeared to have been attacked, or something, Livvy knew this could all be a ruse.

Vernice stumbled forward, tripping in the shallow ditch that separated the road and the cornfield. She fell hard near the back end of one of the cruisers. The side of her face slammed into the ground, but she immediately tried to get up, craning to look at something or someone behind her.

"Stay low, Vernice," Ethan shouted to her. "Try to crawl to this side of the cruiser."

The woman's head whipped up, and she speared Ethan's gaze with those wild eyes. If this was indeed some kind of ruse or trap, then Vernice was very convincing at playing her part.

She managed to lever herself up enough to scramble by the cruiser. Not exactly a safe position since if there was a shooter, he or she could move further down the cornstalks and get to her.

But Livvy was guessing that wouldn't happen.

After all, if the shooter had wanted Vernice dead, she wouldn't have made it this far.

There was another shot, and it slammed into the house right above Ethan's head. Livvy caught onto him again and yanked him down. Since Vernice obviously hadn't fired it, that meant she wasn't the shooter.

Well, not for this round anyway.

But Livvy still didn't trust her. After all, that memory of Vernice peering in through the bathroom window was crystal clear now. The woman had witnessed Livvy's mother being murdered and hadn't done a thing to stop it.

In the distance, Livvy heard the wail of the sirens. She noticed Grace texting someone. No doubt telling them to hold off on their approach until she could give them the all clear.

Whenever that would be.

Livvy kept her attention pinned to Vernice, and she saw the woman manage to lift up her hands. She caught hold of the edge of the tape on her mouth, and inch by inch, she worked it off.

"Help me," Vernice blurted the second she could speak. "He'll kill me. He'll kill all of us."

"Who's *he*?" Ethan demanded, and he thankfully didn't bolt out to try to help Vernice.

She shook her head. "I don't know. A man wearing a ski mask and a heavy coat. He attacked me at my office and drove me here."

Maybe. But Livvy still wasn't going to accept whatever the woman was saying as gospel.

"Does he want you dead because you witnessed Chloe murdering my mother?" Livvy couldn't stop herself from shouting. "You saw everything, and you did nothing to stop her. Nothing!"

A loud sob tore from Vernice's mouth. "Oh, God. You remember. I knew one day you'd remember."

Every muscle in Livvy's body tightened to the point of being painful. The anger roared through her, quickly spinning into a hot rage. Or at least it would have had Ethan not touched her arm. That gentle gesture was enough to remind her to rein in her fury over what Vernice had done.

"She'll pay for that," Ethan murmured, his voice a soothing balm to her tangle of emotions.

Livvy definitely wanted Vernice to pay, and there could be charges brought against her for not reporting a murder that she'd personally witnessed. But Vernice might have been responsible for a whole lot more than that.

"Did you help Chloe kill my mother?" Livvy demanded. And while she wanted to know the answer to that, she also didn't want to get shot by the person who'd fired at them, so she kept watch.

"No." Vernice sobbed again, and it blended with the sounds of pain that Sunny was making. The approaching sirens, too. "I was having an affair with Paul, and Chloe confronted me. She was going to kill me, so I told her it wasn't me sleeping with her husband but rather Belinda. I didn't know she would kill her."

Livvy got a too-clear picture of that. "But you must have known Chloe was going to do something bad because you followed her to the house where my mother had taken me."

Vernice was crying now, the tears streaming down her cheeks. And she eventually nodded. "It was too late for me to stop Chloe. I swear it was too late. Chloe didn't see," she added, her breath hiccupping with the sobs. "Chloe left, and I went in to check on Belinda and you."

There was some movement in the cornfield, just to Vernice's left, and Livvy and Ethan took aim there. She couldn't spot the shooter, but he was possibly moving into position to start firing again.

"You were catatonic or something," Vernice went on. "Not moving, not responding to anything. You were holding the knife, but I took it from you. I figured if Chloe tried to come after me, I could use it as leverage since I believed it would have her prints on it. The knife would be a way of implicating Chloe without me having to admit that I'd seen her murder someone."

Since Chloe's prints hadn't been on the knife, she had likely worn gloves as Franklin had said. Did that mean the rest of what the man had said was also true? If so, where had Hank been when Chloe was murdering Belinda? Vernice hadn't mentioned him, and Livvy wasn't going to question Vernice about that.

Not now anyway.

Because it occurred to her that Vernice could be talking to try to distract them. She could be working with someone who planned to try to kill them all.

There was more movement in the field, but Livvy couldn't be sure if a shift of wind was responsible or if a would-be killer was actually there.

"Let's go with our plan to fire and aim low," she suggested.

This time Grace didn't even hesitate. "Do it. Sunny needs that ambulance now."

Ethan and Livvy adjusted their weapons again. And both fired. The shots were deafening, and they kicked up a spray of dirt at the base of the cornstalks. What they didn't do was cause anyone to run out of there.

However, someone fired back at them.

They dropped lower again, but the bullet hadn't even come close to them. It'd smacked into the exterior wall up near the roof. At first Livvy thought that was because the shooter had been scrambling away.

But no.

More shots came, nonstop now, all of them tearing into the eaves of the roof. And when Livvy looked up, her heart dropped. Because the bullets had weakened a huge chunk of the wood beam, and it was ready to fall right on Ethan and her.

Ethan no doubt saw it, too, because cursing, he pushed her out of the way, moving her closer toward Grace. But their attacker adjusted his shots, and the gunfire began to slam all around them. He was trying to kill them.

And he just might succeed.

"Get under the house," Ethan ordered her.

Livvy wanted to argue. She wanted to stand her ground and help Ethan catch this SOB, but she had to think of the baby. Plus, an argument could play right into their attacker's hands. It could give him the window of opportunity that he needed to finish them off.

She rolled into the narrow opening beneath the house where she was out of the line of fire and also protected if the chunk of roof did indeed fall.

But Ethan wasn't safe.

Neither was Grace.

They had both moved out from their meager cover and had taken aim at the spot in the field where they'd seen that movement. Both of them fired. And fired. They sent two more rounds of bullets into the ground, and at least one of the shots must have hit the roots because one of the stalks toppled to the side.

And that was when Livvy saw him.

A man wearing dark pants, a black shirt and a ski mask. He seemed to freeze for a moment, and then he must have realized he was exposed. He bolted out, darting toward the cruiser, no doubt to use it for cover so he could continue his attack.

He ran fast, leaping across the ditch, and he was only a couple of inches from cover when Ethan fired again.

The man howled in pain, and still moving toward the cruiser, he slapped his left hand over the side of his head. Ethan had obviously hit him, but it wasn't enough to stop him. He dived behind the front end of the cruiser. The moment he landed, he yanked off the ski mask, and Livvy saw the blood dripping from the side of his head. Part of his ear was missing.

And she also saw his face.

Anthony.

He saw Ethan, too. With a feral sound of pain and fury ripping from his throat, Anthony took aim at Ethan and started firing.

# *Chapter Eighteen*

Ethan had no choice but to stay low and hope like hell that Anthony didn't kill him. Because if he managed to do that, it'd make Livvy and Grace easier targets. No way did Ethan intend to let this SOB hurt them and the baby.

"Tell those cops coming to back off," Anthony shouted. "Or I'll gun every one of them down."

Ethan didn't doubt that one bit, and while he couldn't see the main road, he figured both backup deputies and the ambulance were there waiting. Waiting for Grace to let them know it was safe to approach. Right now, the entire area was nowhere near safe.

Not with Anthony out for what he no doubt would call justice.

This attack and the others had to be about avenging his mother's death. Well, probably. It was possible that Anthony had told them a pack of lies about that and he could be doing this for another reason.

Ethan saw the man reloading, and he levered himself up enough to fire a shot at Anthony. It came close, very close, but it ended up ricocheting off the bumper of the cruiser.

Cursing a blue streak, Anthony finished the reload, and Ethan once again had to get belly down onto the ground.

And the shots came.

Mercy, did they.

The bullets were hitting the side of the house, only inches from him and the opening where Livvy had taken cover. Ethan looked at her, meeting her gaze for a split second, and in that blink of time, he saw all the emotions that were in a whirlwind inside him.

He didn't want this for her. He didn't want this for their baby. But at the moment, he didn't have a way to stop it.

"This won't bring back your mother," Ethan shouted, knowing he couldn't reason with Anthony but hoping for the best anyway.

"No, but it'll punish Sunny and Vernice," the man spat out.

So, this *was* about his mother. Considering that Sunny had been the main target of the earlier attacks, it didn't surprise Ethan that Anthony had mentioned her. But he still didn't know why the man wanted her dead. And what the heck did Vernice have to do with Anthony's mother?

"Why Sunny?" Ethan shouted. "She was just a kid when your mother was killed. She had nothing to do with that."

Anthony fired off a few more shots. "Sunny knows why."

"I don't," she yelled back. Obviously, she was still conscious and feeling strong enough to return verbal fire. "Why?" The volume of her voice and her anger actually went up on that single word question.

"You know why," Anthony barked. "The folder that Zadie showed you. She told me she showed you, but Zadie wouldn't give it to me so I could take it to the cops and have that snake, Chloe, arrested."

"I didn't see what was in the folder," Sunny shouted, but her voice dissolved into a hoarse sob. "I swear I didn't see," she repeated. "And I told Zadie to take it to the cops."

"Sure you did," Anthony said, his tone dripping with sarcasm. He didn't believe Sunny, though she was telling the truth.

And that led Ethan to a theory. One that he intended to test right now.

"Anthony," he yelled, "when Zadie didn't give you the file, you killed her, didn't you?"

"Damn right I did. Zadie teased me with that file. She told me all the nasty little details of how Chloe had murdered that woman, Belinda. Stabbing her and putting her in that tub while her kid looked on. That's the person Zadie was protecting. A cold-blooded killer like Chloe. So, I finished them both off. Justice for my mom and for that other woman."

No, it wasn't justice. It was payback. Chloe would have gotten more punishment if she'd been arrested and had to live out the rest of her life in a cage.

"Now Sunny and Vernice have to pay," Anthony went on. "Sunny for being stupid and not turning in her sister for staying quiet about that file. And Vernice because she knew all about my mother's murder. All about it," he shouted.

Ethan glanced at Vernice, who was still sobbing. What she wasn't doing was denying any of it.

"I sneaked into New Hope and was looking for that file when Chloe and Vernice came into Chloe's office," Anthony snarled. "I hid in the records room and heard everything you two conniving witches said. I heard you admit to knowing that Chloe had murdered my mother. You knew and didn't go to the cops."

"Because Chloe would have killed me," Vernice said, her voice shaking so much that it was hard to understand her. "I was pregnant with my daughter, and I couldn't take the risk."

Hell. Ethan refused to feel sorry for this woman. But he did have a question. "Vernice, did you see Chloe kill Ivy, too?"

"No," she was quick to deny. "But Chloe came to my house to wash up afterward. We were friends then. And she wanted to clean up before going home. I saw the blood on her, and when I asked her about it, she said I'd better stay quiet. When I heard about Ivy being in that wreck, I figured out what'd happened."

"Yet you didn't go to the police." Anthony's face was a mask of rage now. "That's why you're going to die. I won't let you get away with it, Vernice. Time to pay, and then Sunny is next in line. Anyone who gets in the way will die right along with them."

Anthony bolted out from the cruiser, not coming at Ethan but rather scrambling to get in front of the cruiser where Vernice was cowering. The man was obviously trying to get into a position where he could shoot her, and he no doubt thought he could dart behind cover in time.

He lifted his gun.

So did Ethan.

Even though Ethan didn't have the best angle for the shot, he was the first to fire. And he didn't miss.

His shot slammed into Anthony's chest, causing the man's body to jerk back just as he pulled the trigger. His shot went wild, blasting into the house right between Ethan and Grace.

And just above where Livvy was.

Ethan cursed, ready to send another shot into Anthony. Ready to do whatever it took to stop him.

Staggering and clutching his chest with his left hand,

Anthony turned, trying to take aim at them, but his body could no longer manage that. He dropped to his knees, his stunned gaze fixed on them. Even then, he tried to take aim again at Vernice, and once more, he failed. Anthony gutted out another of those feral sounds before he crumpled onto the ground, his gun clattering onto the ground.

Ethan was up in a flash, hurrying to Anthony so he could kick the weapon out of reach. Anthony was bleeding and the wound was probably fatal, but that didn't mean the man still wasn't dangerous.

Behind him, Ethan heard the hurried footsteps, and Grace and Livvy stepped up by his side. They, too, had their weapons aimed at Anthony, but it was obvious the man wasn't going anywhere.

"Kill Vernice for me," Anthony said, looking up at Ethan. "If the town rumors are true, you hate her as much as I do."

Ethan's feelings for Vernice hadn't been hatred. Not until now. Not until he'd learned the truth about what she'd done. The woman had witnessed Livvy's mother being murdered and hadn't done a damn thing about it—before or after the fact. Worse, she'd left a traumatized child there with her mother's body. Vernice hadn't had the decency to make an anonymous call to the cops so that someone could have protected Livvy.

Yeah, that made Vernice despicable as far as he was concerned.

"I hate what Vernice did, and what she didn't do. But I won't kill her," Ethan spelled out. "I'll let the justice system hand out her punishment."

Vernice sobbed again, but he ignored her. She wasn't getting a drop of his pity.

"I'll let the deputies and EMTs know it's safe," Grace muttered, stepping aside to make the call.

Ethan glanced at Livvy, at the shell-shocked look on her face, and he wanted to pull her into his arms. Hell, he wanted to kiss her and tell her that everything was going to be all right. But now wasn't the time. Especially since Anthony was likely dying, and this might be their last chance to get some answers.

"Was Franklin involved in any part of your plan?" Ethan asked him.

Anthony laughed, but there was absolutely no humor in it. "Not a chance." He coughed and dragged in a ragged breath. "When I was hooking up with Zadie, I tried to wheedle info out of Franklin, tried to see if he knew anything about what his sister had done, but the man was clueless."

Maybe. Ethan figured it was possible that Franklin could have had an inkling of what his sister had done, but he probably couldn't have imagined that she'd murdered not once but twice. And all because she'd been jealous of her cheating husband.

"Sunny knew," Anthony insisted, the words tumbling out with his breathing.

"I didn't," Sunny protested from behind them.

Ethan glanced back at her. She was on her feet now, but mercy, she had lost a lot of blood. Her whole right side was soaked with it. The moment the EMTs arrived, she'd need to be rushed to the hospital. Grace must have realized that, too, because she hurried out onto the road in front of the house and motioned for the ambulance and cruiser to hurry.

"Why did you stage Zadie's body the way you did in

the tub?" Livvy asked Anthony. Ethan was surprised that she'd managed to keep her voice steady and strong. All cop.

"To frame Chloe," Anthony admitted without any hesitation. "Zadie had told me enough about what was in that file for me to know that's what Chloe had done to that other woman she killed. I figured if Chloe couldn't be punished for the two murders she committed, then she could be punished for this one." He laughed again. "But you cops didn't arrest her. You let her walk around, free as a bird. Well, now she's dead, and I hope she's burning in hell."

Ethan was having a hard time not wishing the same thing. And since Anthony was obviously spilling all, he pushed with another question. "Was it you who hired Hank to go after Sunny?"

"Yeah." Again, no hesitation. "Too bad he failed."

The ambulance and two cruisers pulled to a stop in front of the house, and despite the sounds they were making, Ethan still heard the shuffling movement to his left. He whirled in that direction.

And he saw Sunny pick up Anthony's gun.

"Put that down," Ethan ordered.

But Sunny didn't listen. The woman was trembling from head to toe and there wasn't a drop of color in her face, but she managed to turn the gun on Vernice.

"If you'd turned in Chloe all those years ago, my sister would be alive," she sobbed. "You need to pay for that. You need to die."

"Sunny," Ethan and Livvy shouted at the same time.

If Sunny heard them, she showed no signs of it. She just kept the gun pointed at Vernice, who was now screaming and trying to scramble away. Ethan had no doubt that Sunny was about to pull the trigger, and if so, there was no way Vernice would be able to take cover in time.

He lunged at Sunny, and in the same motion, he tried to push Livvy aside. Out of the possible line of fire.

But he was too late.

Sunny fired. The bullet hit what was left of the wooden fence, ricocheting off a rock or something metal. Splinters flew and chunks of debris flew up, and something, maybe even the bullet itself, sliced across his forehead. Ethan couldn't focus on that though. He couldn't let himself think that Livvy might have been shot. Or soon would be if he didn't get the gun. He just focused on stopping Sunny.

Sunny was clearly focused, too. On killing Vernice. And she took aim again, shifting the gun at Vernice, who was still trying to escape.

Ethan charged at Sunny, ramming into her and clamping his hand on her right wrist. He shoved her arm up into the air. Still, Sunny got off another shot. Then another that he heard ricochet off something. He prayed that Livvy and the others had gotten out of the way.

With all the shouts and the chaos, over Vernice's screams and Grace's orders for everyone to get down, Ethan heard Anthony laugh.

What Ethan didn't hear was any sound from Livvy.

Sunny tried to fight him, tried to use her body to shove Ethan out of the way, and she fired again before he shoved her back, hard, and they tumbled together onto the ground. He tossed his own gun aside so he could use both hands to take control of Sunny's wrist and Anthony's gun. Ethan had to wrench it from her grip, all while Sunny was cursing and sobbing.

Ethan heard the movement around him, and he whirled around again, bracing for the worst.

Fearing the worst.

Terrified that he had lost Livvy and their child.

But he hadn't. Livvy was right there, looking a whole lot stronger than she had just seconds earlier.

The relief hit him hard, robbing him of his breath. He had to take a moment, then another, just to steady himself.

Livvy got him started on the steadiness by touching his arm. Just that. Just a brief touch. Before she then reached down, taking Anthony's gun and handing it off to Grace.

"Sunny, I have to put these on you," Livvy said, cuffing the woman. Sunny didn't protest, didn't attempt to stop her. All the fight had vanished.

Ethan stood, and Livvy and he backed away so the EMTs could rush in to help Sunny.

"It's all right," Livvy murmured to him. "It's over."

She stopped, her eyes going wide, and she cursed under her breath when she looked at him. "Oh, God, Ethan. You've been shot."

# *Chapter Nineteen*

Livvy sat in the chair of the exam room in the ER and watched as the nurse stitched Ethan's head. It was a five-inch gash that went from his temple to the top of his right eyebrow. If the angle of that bullet had been just a fraction off, it could have slammed into his head.

And killed him.

That was why Livvy was still trembling and having trouble leveling herself out. That was why she was cursing herself for not having seen what Sunny had been about to do and stopped her.

"We got lucky," Ethan said, the corner of his mouth lifting into a smile. It wasn't a real one, not heartfelt, and that was probably because he was worried about her, not himself.

But there was no reason to worry about the baby and her. Livvy had already gotten checked out by the doctor and had had yet another ultrasound. Ethan had insisted on that before he would even consent to being stitched up. The doctor had said all was well, and he'd used a similar "You got lucky" remark since she didn't have a scratch on her.

Anthony, Vernice and Sunny definitely hadn't fared so well. Anthony was dead, and the verdict was still out on Sunny's injuries. The woman had been whisked away into surgery as soon as they'd arrived at the hospital. So far, there had been no word on her prognosis or condition. It was entirely possible Anthony would end up claiming another victim.

Vernice also fell into that "to be determined" category. She was in another ER room, being treated for the injuries she'd gotten when Anthony had kidnapped her and taken her to that cornfield.

"All done," the nurse, Abigail Summers, announced, stepping back from Ethan. Livvy knew the young woman, and in a small town where there were often no degrees of separation, she had actually babysat Abigail a time or two.

Abigail aimed a reassuring smile at both of them, and her gaze lowered to Livvy's baby bump. "When are you due?"

"Mid-March," Livvy answered, and while four months still seemed a long time off, she figured it would be here before she knew it.

"And what are you having?" Abigail added, clearing up her stitching supplies.

Livvy looked at Ethan who gave nothing away. "To be determined," she settled for saying.

"I wish you both well. You're free to go," Abigail added to Ethan before she finished gathering her things and walked out.

Ethan immediately got off the exam table, and he went to her. Livvy stood so he could pull her into his arms. Exactly where she needed to be. And yes, the leveling out finally started, though she was certain this latest incident would be giving her nightmares for some time.

"I came too close to losing you," she muttered.

He brushed a kiss on her forehead and held on tight. "I came too close to losing you. Please tell me you'll do desk duty for the rest of the pregnancy."

Livvy didn't intend to give Ethan, or Grace, an argument about that, especially since Grace had already made it clear that field work was off-limits for her until she got back from maternity leave.

She nodded, and while Ethan would still stay fully on the job, she had to say, "And you'll be careful as you can be."

"I always am," he assured her, easing back to meet her gaze.

And to kiss her.

His mouth came to hers, pressing gently and doling out way more pleasure than it should have, considering where they were and what they had just gone through. After he'd pretty much robbed her of her breath and made her feel all warm and pliant, he pulled back and smiled at her.

"To be determined," he repeated. "You closed your eyes again during the ultrasound."

Livvy nodded. "I decided I wanted you to be the one to tell me about the baby's gender." And she hadn't wanted that to happen in front of the ultrasound tech. She wanted that news during a more private moment.

Like now.

Except Livvy needed to tell Ethan something first, and she didn't want to wait to do it. "I told you that I'm in love with you," she started, and then she had to touch her fingers to his mouth to stop him when he tried to interrupt her. "But I want you to know you don't have to do or say anything about that. What I want you to think about instead is more of a...partnership."

His left eyebrow rose, causing the bandage on the other

side of his forehead to lift a little as well. "Please tell me that involves sex. And having you in my bed."

She smiled because this sounded promising. "Sex is on the table," she admitted and then laughed when she heard how suggestive that sounded. "I was thinking more of us maybe moving in together after the baby comes. And you don't have to give me an answer now. Just give it some thought because that could be the easiest way for us to co-parent."

He frowned, causing her heart to drop. No, no, no. She'd pushed too much, too soon. Ethan wasn't ready for this kind of arrangement.

After too many snail-crawling moments, he finally opened his mouth to respond, but the knock on the door stopped him.

"It's me," they heard Grace say, and she opened the door and peered in. She saw the way they were standing, with Livvy still in Ethan's arms, and she smiled. "Glad to see you're both doing well."

They were, physically anyway, but Livvy could feel that broken heart of hers coming on.

"How's Sunny?" Ethan asked.

Livvy was thankful he'd spoken and filled the silence. She didn't want Grace to pick up on the gloom and doom that had to be coming off her. Besides, she wanted to know how Sunny was doing as well.

Grace gathered in a long breath. "She's out of surgery and is expected to make a full recovery." She paused, groaned and shook her head. "I'll have to charge her, though, with the shooting. A good lawyer will argue diminished capacity because of her injury and grieving her sister's death, and she might get off."

Livvy hoped she did. She couldn't condone Sunny's actions of trying to kill Vernice, but she understood being overwhelmed by a horrible situation. Sunny had lost her twin sister and had nearly been killed twice. Most people would break under circumstances like that.

"What about Vernice?" Ethan asked.

"She's already been treated and released," Grace explained. "Rory is taking her to the station, where he'll get her statement. She'll be charged with obstruction of justice for bringing in that knife. The statute of limitations is up on her failing to report a crime, but I'll see if there are any other charges we can bring against her."

Livvy hated that Vernice hadn't turned in Chloe. Sunny had been right about that—if Vernice had reported Belinda's murder, then Zadie would be alive. Chloe, too. Sunny wouldn't have been injured, and the attacks wouldn't have happened.

But there was a silver lining of sorts here.

All of this had caused Livvy to remember, and while they were horrible memories, at least now she knew the truth about what'd happened.

"How are you dealing with all of this?" Grace asked, volleying glances at both of them but her attention settling on Livvy.

Livvy had to take a breath, too. "Part of it—to be determined. I'd like to find out what happened to my mother's body so I can give her a proper burial."

Grace nodded. "I've already called out a team to search the area around the old house. If her remains are there, we'll find them."

Good, because that would be a start. "I'd also like to learn more about my mother. Maybe talk to some of the other surrogates or New Hope employees who might have known her."

Grace nodded again and hiked her thumb in the direction of the waiting room. "You might be able to get some of those answers from Franklin. He showed up here about fifteen minutes ago, asking to speak to you. If you don't want to see him, I'll tell him to get lost."

"No, I'll speak to him." Though Livvy didn't intend for it to be a long conversation. More like scratching the surface for now. Because at the moment her priority was finishing her conversation with Ethan.

"All right," Grace said, stepping out of the way and then following them to the door. "Let me know if there's anything I can do to help. In the meantime, you're both off duty. I don't want to see either of you in the station for at least the next three days. If you need more time than that to sort things out, just let me know."

"Thank you," Livvy and Ethan replied, and while Livvy couldn't speak for him, she would take every hour of those three days. She needed the rest and the time to process everything that'd happened.

When the three of them made it to the waiting room, Livvy immediately saw Franklin stand up from one of the chairs. He didn't have that cocky look he'd sported when they had first visited him at New Hope. Just the opposite. He appeared to be exhausted and devastated.

Franklin didn't walk toward them. He just waited for them to come to him.

"I'm sorry," he said. "So very sorry for what my sister did to you and your mother. Your mother was a good woman, and she didn't deserve what happened to her."

Livvy had had a decent rein on any tears, but that caused some to pool in her eyes. She blinked them back because she was afraid if she started crying, she wouldn't be able to stop.

"I came by to tell you how sorry I am," Franklin explained. "And to let you know that I'm closing New Hope and transferring the current clients and surrogates to other facilities." He took out a small envelope from his pocket and handed it to Livvy. "I also wanted to give you this. I found it last night when I was going through some of my things."

Livvy couldn't help but remember the last time Franklin had given her something. It'd been that file with the horrific details of her mother's murder. That was why her hand was trembling and why her stomach had tightened to knots.

Ethan reached out, took the envelope from her and looked at her, silently asking her if she wanted him to open it. Livvy nodded, and she held her breath, waiting.

There was only one item inside, and when he took it out, Livvy saw that it was a photo.

"It was taken in the garden at New Hope," Franklin muttered. "I thought you'd like to have it."

Livvy heard his words but didn't respond. That was because her attention was on the picture—a smiling woman holding the hand of a little girl. It was her and her mother.

There was no fear and terror like the memories of them cowering on the stairs. Or them running to get away from Chloe. No. This was a happy moment. And more. So much more. Livvy could see the love in her mother's eyes.

Love for her child.

Livvy felt one of those tears spill down her cheek, and she didn't try to blink back any others. She just let them come. Not tears of grief and despair. But of this moment that she remembered. The warmth of her mother's love.

That precious time they'd had together. Chloe might have ended her mother's life, but she couldn't take away these memories.

"Thank you," Livvy managed to say.

Franklin was crying, too, but like her tears, she thought there was a tinge of happiness to his. "Call me anytime you want to talk about Belinda or your time at New Hope."

Livvy nodded, and wiping his eyes, Franklin muttered a goodbye and turned to leave.

Grace cleared her throat, and Livvy realized her eyes were misty, too. But she smiled and patted Livvy's arm. "Go home, you two, and get started on that downtime," she added as she walked away.

Livvy stared at the photo several moments longer and then looked at Ethan. The word *home* was repeating in her head, and she wanted to work that out with him before they left. So, she took his hand and led him back into the treatment room where he'd gotten his stitches.

She shut the door, turned to him and was about to launch into a full-scale apology for dumping that *I'm in love with you* on him. But she didn't get the chance.

Because Ethan kissed her again.

And there was nothing gentle about this one. It was hard, hungry and all heat. It slid through her like wildfire and kept on spreading until Livvy was reasonably sure she could no longer speak.

But Ethan could, and he proved that when he finally pulled away from her.

"I'm not going to backpedal on what you said about being in love with me," he blurted. "Ditto for your offer on that partnership thing about us moving in together. I want that, and I want the *I love you*."

Livvy was certain she looked surprised because she was. Surprised, aroused and incredibly relieved. "You want the *I love you*?" she questioned.

"Damn straight I do. And I want to give it right back to you." He took hold of her shoulders and looked her straight in the eyes. "I'm in love with you, Livvy. And I love you, too," he added, stooping down to drop a kiss on her baby bump. "And I want it all. The love, the partnership, living together and marriage. By the way, in case you didn't catch it, that's a proposal."

"I caught it," she managed to say. Livvy also managed to say something else. "And my answer is yes. Because I want it all, too."

Ethan smiled, lighting up that gorgeous face of his, and he dragged her back to him for another kiss. One to seal the deal. And to heat up every inch of her.

"Let's take this home," he suggested, still smiling with his mouth against her.

"Great idea. Home, and then I can haul you off to bed."

Ethan stole another kiss as they headed out of the room and toward the exit. "And after some great sex, maybe we can come up with wedding plans. Maybe even baby names."

All of that sounded perfect, and she looked up at him as they walked outside and to the cruiser. "A gender reveal," she muttered, getting behind the wheel while he took shotgun. "You think this is the right time and the right place for that?"

Another smile. Another kiss. This one even hotter than the last one. "Perfect time and place," he assured her.

He pulled back, and still smiling, Ethan murmured, "What do you think about the name Ben?"

"A boy," she whispered, letting the joy flood through her.

Livvy got an instant flash of images. New memories that they'd make together. Happy ones with the family that she would have with Ethan and their son.

* * * * *